About the Author

Ingrid Lynch taught school for over forty years. It was only when she retired, she began to write. At first, she wrote hastily – but now she is more deliberate; in everything she writes, there is her theme that true Americans are champions whenever they try to correct those things that are wrong, to help those who are helpless. Those who think they are losers, who rise to the challenge of being champions, are the heart of America.

The Arroyo Man

Ingrid Lynch

The Arroyo Man

Olympia Publishers
London

www.olympiapublishers.com
OLYMPIA PAPERBACK EDITION

Copyright © Ingrid Lynch 2023

The right of Ingrid Lynch to be identified as author of
this work has been asserted in accordance with sections 77 and 78 of
the Copyright, Designs and Patents Act 1988.

All Rights Reserved

No reproduction, copy or transmission of this publication
may be made without written permission.
No paragraph of this publication may be reproduced,
copied or transmitted save with the written permission of the publisher,
or in accordance with the provisions
of the Copyright Act 1956 (as amended).

Any person who commits any unauthorised act in relation to
this publication may be liable to criminal
prosecution and civil claims for damage.

A CIP catalogue record for this title is
available from the British Library.

ISBN: 978-1-80439-293-5

This is a work of fiction.
Names, characters, places and incidents originate from the writer's
imagination. Any resemblance to actual persons, living or dead, is
purely coincidental.

First Published in 2023

Olympia Publishers
Tallis House
2 Tallis Street
London
EC4Y 0AB

Printed in Great Britain

Dedication

For all those so different or so ugly they feel they aren't able to live with others.

I know you've heard things about the Irish. You know, how all their wars are merry and all their songs are sad. I've read there were lads from Ireland only months arrived in the states who joined the military and ended up with Custer. I bet they weren't too glad to be with him at the Little Big Horn. I'm an American of Irish descent, and I've spent most of my adult life in the military. I've never enjoyed any war I've experienced. And the sorrows in my life—I'm not singing about those. However, it is true, I think, that the Irish turn up all over the world with the darndest people. That much is true.

I'm Patrick Monahan, and my dad was Liam Monahan. In Dad's case, he joined up with old Franz Gephardt, a man older and smarter than he was. That was in Dutch Harbor, Alaska, just before the Second World War.

Back in those days, Dutch Harbor was one of the busiest ports in the world. Maybe it still is. There were freighters from everywhere in that harbor. Old Franz had just enough money to buy a freighter older than it should have been, one everyone felt was ready to be scrapped.

Instead, he and my dad managed to make the *Alvardo Cabrel* seaworthy. Dad said Franz was stubborn, that he would never give up, but he sure wasn't rich.

"The two of us, we had to do everything. There wasn't anybody else," Dad said.

That included diving to repair the vessel's hull. The two of them worked on that for about two years. At the same time, they worked as hired hands. I was just a little toddler then, and I don't remember Dutch Harbor, but I feel as if I do remember it because Dad talked about it so much. It must have been very hard going for them in those days.

"On the top deck, Franz had stuff spread out all over the

place. If it had anything to do with electricity, he was working on it. It was like his lab or his workshop up there." Dad told me it was surprising how many electrical problems you could run into on a freighter. It was up to Dad to keep things running smoothly when they finally were able to hire crew and set sail. In the meantime, Franz was turning into a serious communications inventor.

It was low frequency radio waves that intrigued Franz the most. I don't know how much formal education Franz had. All I know is that he began working on communicating with and locating submarines. There began to be patents. There were lots of them as the war began, and lawyers who protected such things as intellectual property as well as the inventions themselves. They knew all about such things as registering patents and starting up corporations. Things were looking up. Others were working for Franz and my dad. No two men ever deserved it more.

I remember Franz from those earliest days when he suddenly became the heart of a new corporation. Bushy eyebrows, he had those, over dark, serious eyes. And he had lots of hair. He was tall, and as a child, I was a little afraid of him. Maybe that was because he was wrapped up in his work. Telecommunications was a field opening wide, and Franz had found his niche.

He moved himself, his wife Mickey (Minerva), and his little boy Franz Junior to the northern part of Delaware, a state friendly to corporations and banks. Dad took my mom and me right along with them to live close by.

I never felt Dad was happy with that move. It was a step down for him. Now he was just the driver who took Franz back and forth to Wilmington corporate offices and provided security for the estate Franz called home. My dad, with his blue eyes and wide smiling face, had the soul of a sailor. He'd spent so much time on the *Alvardo Cabrel*, running things, it was hard for him to change. There were two other freighters now, but it was that first one Dad loved. Even in Delaware, Dad could contact a home office in Alaska and get patched through to the *Cabrel* wherever she was. He stayed in touch with that freighter almost every week. He was so proud she was still working. He couldn't let go.

***

It was a lovely place where my schooling began and ended. Living there were well-known writers and artists. There were lots of white-fenced pastures and horses, and pheasants sometimes ran across the road in front of your car. Tree-lined lanes led up to impressive doorways. It was beautiful and private, this world of old Franz Gephardt. Maybe Franz wasn't so crazy about it, but his wife loved it. Franz Senior wasn't much of a social person.

"He'd have me pull over all the time after he'd been away for a few days, just to ask questions. Were there any of those play-boy types hanging around Mickey? Had anybody been allowed near his lab or his library? When he was away, had those lab doors been unlocked?" Dad said Mickey was oblivious to anybody except Franz, and the answers were always no.

"Who could tell if anybody'd been in that lab? It looked like a storm hit in there. But he knew where everything was. Quit talking to him about being neat." Dad and Franz were fast friends, and my father could laugh about it, but the truth was

Franz was a grumpy character who didn't care about other people. There were a lot of people, not all of them Americans, who wanted to talk to him. U.S. government people knew of him, too, and some of those drove to Wilmington every day, parked, talked, and then took the train to D.C. They commuted back and forth every day, and some of them were very important. Politicians wanted to talk, too. Franz didn't care.

Part of Dad's job was to keep people away from him. Nothing mattered except work to Franz. It was rumored in those days his experiments had taken some strange turns, and that was why he was so secretive. But that was just talk. If it was about communications, Franz was on it. I think Dad and Franz Junior were the only ones allowed in that lab and library.

You'd think that Franz Junior and I would be good friends, since we were the same age and attended the same schools. That wasn't the case. There have never been two students less likely to be friends. While my dad was average in height, I towered over him. Old Franz and his wife were both tall, but their son was a lot shorter. He was what I would call a "pretty boy". Darkly handsome, that's what comes to mind. His eyes were almost purple, making girls dream of him. His hands were what made me pause. They were pampered. That's how I felt about him, that he would be of such an introverted nature he'd be impossible to please.

That's what kept me from wanting to know him well. He had few friends because that was what suited him. He left school each day and entered the world of his father's lab. I wasn't a part of that world. I was into sports and girls, particularly that one girl I'd been in love with and protecting since third grade. I never was in the big estate house, and it didn't bother me. Nobody was cruel to me or said, "Don't you dare come in here." It just didn't interest me.

Not that Mickey couldn't be cruel. Later on, I heard what happened when her grown son first brought into the house a young woman named Madge who made the mistake of being offensive. She came out of a bathroom to announce hotly that if this were her house, there'd be some hand towels in there. Mickey went and got some, put them into the offender's hands, and then told her where she could stick 'em after she used them. Some people didn't get asked to visit again. Mickey was friendly with everybody, but if you angered her, she wouldn't forget it. Neither would you.

***

After Mickey's death, Old Franz decided to leave the East. His grown son could take over. He'd trained him to do that. Franz wanted a simpler way of life. He said he could breathe better in the foothills of Arizona. I always suspected the real reason he chose Arizona was because there would be fewer people there. That might have been part of it, anyway. My mom and dad moved right along with him. Force of habit, I guess. I was on my own by then.

After Franz died, my parents died not long after. My retirement from the army came at about the same time. It was when I inspected their home that I decided I wanted to live in it myself. It's a nice piece of property, about seven acres, with Franz's home at the farther end of it and my parents' smaller place at the lower end of its downward slope. The property ends where there are some neighbors and roads with sidewalks. I became owner of the lower half of it. I felt at home at once, possibly because all the things my mom and dad possessed were still in the house. Dad's work gloves are on a shelf in the car port. I use their kitchen utensils, sleep in their bed, and walk on their area rugs. I simply moved in, as if I was visiting them on leave as I once did. I'm comfortable with that. I especially love their garden. I think it was the Romans who said all you need is a library and a garden. It's easy to feel that way here.

It's the covered bricked patio I like best. I can sit out there in the evening, smoking a cigar and having a beer. There's usually a breeze. The heavens are crowded with stars.

There's a dirt service road that leads past the low wall encircling the back garden. It continues up to what was Franz's house. On the other side of that road, there's an arroyo. That's a deep rocky ditch that carries off flood water from the torrential rains Arizona sometimes endures, even though most of the year is dry here.

That part of living here, the part without rain, is disconcerting, but with drip irrigation the garden does well. There are big hawks that carry off small pets, and there are those unfriendly coyotes and bobcats, and also those snakes, but so far, my little Scottish terrier and I have been doing just fine here. Living alone, just the little dog and myself, isn't new. I've never risked myself in marriage. Somehow, I've arrived at this place in one piece, on the verge of old age.

My view out over the garden wall gives me an advantage. Inside the garden, the ground is on a higher level than outside the wall. If I'm inside the garden, the wall rises to my waist. But if I'm standing on the dirt service road, looking in from that vantage point, the wall is up to my chin. Anyone speaking to you is looking up; you are looking down at him or her if you are inside the garden. I should stop thinking about having an "advantage". There's no military advantage or disadvantage here. It's all very peaceful. Nothing exciting is going to happen. It takes some getting used to.

***

One evening, as I was sitting on the patio, I got a glimpse of a man walking in that dry arroyo. I could see only the head of that person, and he couldn't see me at all, not only because of my being higher, but also because of a climber rose that hid me from his view. It was strange how that large head went along so smoothly, almost like a balloon. The arroyo's bottom is full of rocks, but earlier, when I first moved in, I'd looked down into it from the service road, and I could see in the arroyo a little path winding along one side just above those rocks, so he must have been walking there. He wore a brimmed cap with material hanging down from it, so his neck and ears were protected from the sun. He was wearing sunglasses. I assumed it was a man, for no woman I knew would have walked there.

Usually, my Scottie, Stinker, would have been barking, but instead, he was peering out through a small crack in the garden wall, and he was quiet. Stinker's been with me all over the world, just about, and he always lets me know when someone is close by, but this time he was quiet. I thought that was strange.

Sometimes I think like Stinker. One could do worse than to think like a dog. I watch his nose. One of the stinkiest places I ever was in was 'Nam. Get into jungle just a few hundred yards and you're not going to be heard no matter how loud you yell. And you can't see the enemy. Even when I ended up in government buildings with endless paperwork, I always just had to go outside, like my dog, to seek out the perimeters of the place and figure out how one could defend it. Or escape from it.

So one of the things I like about living here is there's a lot of open land. You can see what's ahead and all around you. There are observatories on mountain tops nearby. One day I'm going to get up to one of those places and view the area from far above. That's even better. Stinker's nose would love the smells from there.

I have mixed feelings about the service roads that run behind and alongside houses. I have walked along this dirt service road all the way up to what was Franz's house and looked out into the desert to the mountains beyond. What complicates service roads are the other little service roads that connect into each other.

When I saw the man in the arroyo, I noticed he was wearing sunglasses, but he was walking into the east, away from the sun, and the sun was very close to setting, so I decided when he started out, it was a sunny day, and he'd been walking for some time. He was in that arroyo because he didn't want to meet anyone walking or driving along the service roads. All he had to do was duck down to go unnoticed. So he was up to something, probably. I got one more glimpse of him as he progressed upward, but he could have been going anywhere on those connecting service roads or simply on up to Franz's house and even past that. He aroused curiosity and a little suspicion. He was one of the things that could mean danger.

I told myself I was now living where everything different or new didn't have to mean it was dangerous. Even so, both Stinker and I were startled when a little while later, we heard a short cry of alarm, a sort of feminine scream, followed by loud words, an argument of some sort, coming from what had been Franz's place. Those sounds ended as quickly as they began, and then there was silence.

Stinker and I listened for a while to see if there would be more noise, but all was silent, so finally we went to bed. I had supposed Franz's place was empty, but it could have been sold or rented even before I arrived here. I shouldn't let myself get alarmed at every turn. It's peaceful here; I have to keep reminding myself.

***

Next morning, curiosity got the best of me. I decided to put Stinker on his leash for a short walk up that service road toward Franz's place just to see if there was anybody there. There's only one other service road that cuts in and joins the one I was traveling on, along the same road where the man was when I last saw him the night before. Franz bought a sizable piece of property, and there weren't any houses between the one I have and the one he'd lived in. I figured those voices must have come from there or near there.

I was joined along the way by Carol Bentley and her dog. And I must add a word about women here. I'm usually not trusting women who show up anywhere near me with "favors" of any kind. Maybe you know the kind I mean. They bring their casserole dishes to your door. That's fine if there's been a death in the family, or if there's been a divorce and the man doesn't know how to cook, or somebody's sick, something like that. But if none of those things are true, if your only qualification for that casserole supper is that you're single, then she's looking for something she lost or needs in her life. In that case, not me. Not interested

Carol's different. She's a neighbor who showed up at the patio wall one evening. She offered to take Stinker for a brief walk along with her own dog. When I said mine got enough exercise just running around the back garden, she said I shouldn't be silly, turning down a free walker. I took offense at that and said he couldn't take a long walk. His legs were so short. He wasn't used to long walks. She suggested I take a look at her dog, so I leaned over the wall, and there was a sorrowful sort of basset hound sitting there who was slung even closer to the ground than Stinker and whose legs might be even shorter than my dog's.

"Ah, we don't do long walks," she said. "My husband started calling this dog a silly name, and it stuck. We're not proud. We're not athletic." When I handed Stinker over to her, she was impressed. "Oh, he's purebred," she said.

As she left with the two dogs, she added, "My dog says he doesn't care about that fancy stuff. Me, neither, Fatty Pants," she added, speaking to her dog.

She did mention a husband. So I relaxed a lot, and sometimes I do walk Stinker now, and sometimes she'll stop by and take him for a walk. She used the word "purebred" to describe a dog, and that impressed me. It's easy to walk along with her and Stinker and Fatty Pants.

As we approached the house that had been home to old Franz, I could see there was a luxury car parked outside that place. It had a license plate from Delaware. I got a feeling this could mean trouble. It made me stop and turn around. Carol wanted to know what the problem was. I made up some excuse. I just didn't want to get closer. Stinker finished his walk with her, but I retreated. You don't see many license plates from Delaware. It's a small state, and I guess the people living there don't travel much. But here was a license plate from Delaware, and what were the chances of that?

***

You should know some things about my house. It's not a living room for women, not so much. Everything here is for the comfort of a man. That was my mom's way. The sofa is kind of old, but it's longer and it's comfortable, and my length loves it. The easy chairs are overstuffed, and the ash trays are large enough a cigar fits in them. There are smoke trails smudged up the front of the fireplace, and that doesn't bother me. On each side of the fireplace there's a set of French doors. The pair on the far side, on my left, but to the right for anyone approaching the house, hasn't been opened for years. I doubt anyone could open them. I use the other side as my front door. That's on the service road and arroyo side of the house. That side opens all right. There's no doorbell. There's some kind of gauzy see-through curtains hanging on those French doors. Probably that stuff has been hanging there for fifty years. I'm not big on replacing curtains, so that suits me just fine. I usually pull into the car port, where it's shady, and go back into the covered patio, also shady, to enter the house by the sliding glass doors at the rear of the house. Then I'm in the breakfast room, kitchen area, just where I want to be if I'm carrying a few groceries in. I don't think any of the windows in this house have been opened in years. When I moved in, I got the air conditioner replaced because it gets really hot in the summer, and I don't mess with opening any windows. Let them stay just the way they are; that's my reasoning. I'm usually at the back of the house anyway, sitting on the patio. Or I'm sprawled on the sofa watching the big TV I have installed on the fireplace wall.

***

I was sitting on the patio when I heard knocking on the French doors. It was really loud knocking when I finally paid attention to it. I had been reading. When I went to the front of the house, I could see through the curtains two people knocking on the wrong doors. I opened my side and gathered them in.

"Why didn't you hear us?" one of them grumbled loudly. I saw this was a man and a woman, and the woman was the Madge I'd seen once and heard about. I saw her at a gathering in Mickey's garden. On that occasion, I walked around to the back of the house, just checking things out, and a couple of the biggest generators I ever saw were back there. I also saw Franz Junior and Madge being more than a little friendly. It was shortly after that I went back into the military for good and made it my career.

Now that same woman was at my door, older but still stylishly the same. She was Franz Junior's mistress, so the scowling man with her had to be him. I wouldn't have recognized him. I felt superior for a heady moment, for I'm still slim, and this man was overweight and no longer attractive. He was also impatient.

"You're Patrick Monahan, right." It wasn't really a question. I nodded. "My father depended on yours for security. You can help me."

What he wanted were cameras, security cameras. He wanted protection from anyone coming at him from the mountains or from the direction of the arroyo and service road. He wanted me to get them installed and to be quick about it.

"You'll have to be more specific. Do you want cameras that are video cameras or give off alarms or—"

"Everything. I'll pay for everything. I want one installed at your place, too. I'll give you my card; my phone number's on it. If you get a hit, then you'd call me, and I'd have a warning. I'll need your phone number. I'll give you one thousand a month if you do that."

"Why do you need all this, anyway?" I asked, and there was a pause.

The woman, Madge, jumped in with an explanation. "It was him! Him! He came to our house!"

Immediately Franz put his hand up at her mouth, a gesture that said stop. Now.

"We've had an intruder," he said. He gave me his card. It had his phone number on it.

I was flustered. This wasn't something I wanted to do. Our fathers had been best friends, nonetheless. That meant a lot. Besides, obviously the "HIM" had to have something to do with the person I'd seen in that arroyo. I put my phone number on a stick-um page and gave it to him. I was curious enough to cooperate.

"No, I don't want your money," I said. "You'll pay for the equipment and the workers who install the cameras, and that's all. This will take a couple of weeks at least to be delivered."

"That long?"

"I have to send for what you want. Can't be rushed. When it comes, it comes."

I would live to regret giving him my phone number. Here were two of my least favorite people in the world. Madge was looking around critically at my humble living room, moving away from the French door where she'd entered as if one of those ancient curtains might touch her arm. I paused for a moment, thinking about the difference between those who say "dad" and those who say "father". But they were soon gone, leaving me to wonder if I had gotten myself into something I would regret.

I brushed aside any doubts, for I wanted to learn more about the man in the arroyo.

I couldn't remember Madge's last name. Franz Junior must have met her when she had a business career in the corporate offices in Wilmington, Delaware. On the occasion I last saw her, I felt she was a person who would be as hard to please as he was. She was stylish but false in her style: false eyelashes, false hairpieces, false nails, false boobs, looking like a manikin in a woman's shop until she moved and you realized she was a live woman, that sort of thing.

I have my own idea of beauty, true beauty. I think it's the face we're most familiar with that becomes truly beautiful to us. Once we know the real person behind the face, we love it. The rest of the world might find that face ugly, but that's not so for us. In my years of duty, I've seen faces of all kinds. Twice, those were the faces of the dying. The world might find a face handsome or beautiful, but behind that face, so often there's nothing. What I find to be true in the military is that behind the faces of those I think of as being truly beautiful, there's always one shining thing: Honor.

***

It took longer than I'd thought for the equipment to come. It took two and a half weeks for it all to arrive. During that time, I got two cranky phone calls from Franz Junior complaining about how slow things were going. But once they got started, the workers and I got everything done and cleaned up in three days. At my place, I already had a sensor light at the end of the house near the paved road and sidewalk. It wasn't a camera. It simply came on when anything was stirring on the service road or arroyo. Now, on the same side of the house, concentrating on the service road and the arroyo, I installed the nicest sensor camera. I put it in myself. It looked for all the world like a knob of bark, like a part of a tree, and you had to look hard to see the lens. It was a little work of art. It would take a photo whenever it detected movement, followed by a second photo split seconds later. It worked silently, and inside the house, it would alarm to let you know it found something. Then on a screen, the photos it took would appear in color. I put that little camera on the trunk of a western magnolia growing alongside the house. Daytime or nighttime, that setup was supposed to work, and I tested it with a fellow walking past it on the service road. It worked perfectly. It put on its screen a better color picture than what I was getting on my TV.

At Franz's place, we installed two cameras (at his insistence) on the eastern end of his house. One came on once every eight hours to snap photos of the desert and the far-off mountains. The other came on only when it sensed nearby movement and took photos in black and white. That was a waste of money, for nobody was going to come over such open land to intrude on him. The other two cameras, on the other end of the house, trained on the arroyo and the road, operated pretty much in the same way, but they gave a printed report whenever they caught anything on film, and one of them was a video camera. They were tested and were working perfectly when we left them. Franz paid for everything, just as he had promised.

And then we waited.

I was almost hoping somebody would come along so all the

cameras could prove themselves, especially the pretty little thing on that tree.

I couldn't help myself. I suggested to Franz Junior that he could talk to our local police chief about whatever his problem was with this intruder, and then our local cops would look out for him. They could help him.

He didn't even look at me. "No," he said casually. "Certainly not." So he didn't want local attention. That was interesting.

***

It was evening, getting dark. I was in the kitchen when I realized the sensor light at the front of the house had just come on. Usually that light stays on for a while, but not this time. As I looked in its direction, I saw it go off immediately. Then that little camera on the tree started its alarm, a soft *blip blip* noise. I hurried to the screen I'd put on a desk under the window near that camera, pulled up a chair and plopped myself in it, waiting breathlessly. That camera provided its own light for night shots. There was a soundless flash of light and, with it, two clicks. I knew that camera had taken two shots. I watched the small screen come alive.

Astonished, I saw it turn gray and then black. My camera had failed. I couldn't believe it. Here I was, thinking I was unseen and in charge, behind closed blinds. I got an uneasy feeling somebody or something out there was running things.

Suddenly that little screen came alive. Two photos appeared. The camera had done its job after all. Good work then, camera.

I was jubilant, moving closer to the screen. He was in the

arroyo again. The first photo showed a slightly startled face, half turned toward the lens. The second one showed a face full on, looking at me with a shy sort of smile. I could see signs of faintly reddish hair from under the brim of his cap. The person was a male, much younger than I am. The sunglasses, this time, were on top of his cap.

The most interesting thing about both photos was that the person was an albino. His skin was chalk-white, contrasting with the darker colors of the arroyo behind him. The skin around the eyes was a little darker, a shade of gray, and the eyes weren't pink; they were also gray. I got the feeling of sorrow from those eyes, although the second photo showed an expression of pleasant surprise.

As I studied those two photos, I had a pretty good idea of who this young albino was, even if I didn't know his name.

***

Where was Stinker all this time? I found him on the patio, his nose once again concentrating on that crack in the wall. I made a mental resolution to fill in that crack. His stumpy tail was wagging. I took out the card Franz had left with me and studied it for a moment, and then I decided I'd let Stinker call it on this one.

"All right, I won't call." I let it go. Maybe I wanted to see if there would be angry voices coming from that direction again. There was only silence and darkness. I gave up and went to bed.

There wasn't going to be any sleep. I tossed and turned restlessly. I have put all the cruelest things, the things that hurt me most, in mental boxes I just ignore, but tonight some of those were opened. I visited again anguish about the love of my life, about awaking moaning because I dreamed she was beside me in the bed, when she was lost forever. Overhead, there were battalions of innocent stars in a clear sky over my poor little house, but memories of Jenny rained down on me all night.

Eventually, I slept, only to dream of things moving in a line. Perhaps it was a string of wolves about to savage some poor vulnerable thing. When things move in single file, it's always horrible. Whether it's men or wolves, or chimps, it's bad. It turned out, in my dream, I was moving single file with other men over rough country, and then I heard the pounding of artillery and shots.

Stinker's barking awoke me. It was mid-morning. It was a knocking on that front French door that I was hearing.

It was the woman, Madge. She was frightened, and she wanted to come in, but I blocked her from doing that. I was barely awake, and I needed some coffee, at least, to deal with her. She wanted me to come to their place to check the cameras. She was sure their intruder had been around again just before Franz Junior left, and the cameras hadn't been working. At least nothing was warning her, and she was alone there, for Franz was in Delaware. He often went there for corporate meetings, and she was afraid when she was left alone.

"I know that man was near last night," she said. "I could just *feel* it." I promised her I would go check on the cameras a little later on. After all, my own camera failed.

When I checked, there was nothing wrong with the cameras. She was unhappy with that.

A few days later, after Franz returned, he made the same request, and this time, when I checked, sure enough, there had been a lapse in the cameras' coverage. I couldn't explain that. For about half an hour, the cameras weren't in service. Franz was furious. There must have been a power failure. There wasn't any power failure at my place, so close by. That was puzzling.

I wondered why on earth those two were so on edge, anyway. Nobody was trying to break into their house or was peeping into the windows or playing pranks. Something was deeper than that, and it was bothering them a lot.

I tried to put it out of my mind. I had, by God, done my part. Maybe they should consider getting a guard dog. They should have done that in the first place, probably. Would have worked better and have been a whole lot cheaper.

***

About three weeks or so passed rather peacefully. There were no phone calls from Franz Junior or his Madge, and I began to feel hopeful those two had settled down. I would hear their voices arguing from time to time, so I knew their partnership wasn't pleasant, but aside from Franz slipping away in his car occasionally to go get a few beers (I supposed) or spend the night in some motel to get away from her, it was better than it had been.

I had been putting some dishes away in the kitchen, and now that I was done, I silently stepped outside to the patio. Stinker was at the far end of the garden, where the huge rambler rose covered so much of the wall. He was on his hind legs, his paws and face on the wall, peering over. Because it was night now, I wondered what in the heck he could be looking at. I got chills when I realized there were fingers petting my dog's head, patting him, and there was a voice whispering to him. There was someone standing on the other side of that wall, face to face with Stinker. Someone was hidden by all the rose branches, and I couldn't see his face, but I bet he could see mine any old time he wanted to if he stood quietly behind a rose bush and a wall whenever he felt like it.

"If you snatch my dog and drag him off, I'll surely kill you," I said, and I meant it.

There was no way I could go over that wall and catch any younger person who grabbed Stinker, and I knew it.

No such thing was necessary. There was sudden activity there, for Stinker knew from my voice I was angry, and he turned and fled into the house, leaving fluttering hands and a face I could see.

"Oh, no, no—I wouldn't—I would never! Please! Please! Let me explain!" There was real panic on the face of the young albino man I'd seen before on the camera screen. "You don't know me, but I think my mom—my mother—knew you. I don't mean harm... no danger, not from me."

I stood silently, looking him over. His eyes affected me the most, but he was striking in other ways. His ears and his head were rather large, and the fingers on his hands were longer than mine. He gestured at the wall before him.

"If I could sit here to talk—"

"Yeah. Do that."

He surprised me when I saw him spring up through the rambler and perch easily on the rim of the garden wall.

"It's just that sometimes I saw your dog peering over, and I started talking to him. I never could—wasn't allowed— to have a dog. And I heard you talking to him, calling him by his name. Then one time, I saw you coming out of the house, and I saw your face, and I recognized you from the photo my mom had on her desk. I know you don't know me, but I think I know you."

"Wrong. I think you're the son of Franz Gephardt Junior."

Hearing that, he was a little startled, enough so that he looked away for a moment. "Yes. Not happy about that, not really." Now he looked at me directly, and I realized what had struck me about his eyes. He had his mother's gray eyes. This was Jenny's child.

Something in me sagged as if a sorrow moved forward and softened me a little. He seemed to sense that.

"Why would you name a nice dog *Stinker,* anyway?" he asked softly.

"You wouldn't have to ask if you had a puppy pooping in the house," I said. "Even when he knew better, the name stuck with him."

"But that's not his real name."

"No. On his papers, he has an official name. A fancy one. It's like a racehorse has a name he runs under on the track, but he has a barn name, what he's really called."

"My mother told me your name. That was a photo of her dear friend, she told me. She gave me your name as my middle name. That's on my birth certificate. My middle name is Patrick."

Jenny had given my name to him as part of his identity. Some part of me was staggering under knowing that.

"When I was little, we would play Patty Cake, Patty Cake, Baker's Man. She'd say I was Patty Cake Patrick, Patty Cake Pat. I guess that was my name when we played that."

I was close to choking, trying to swallow.

"What's Stinker's fancy name?"

"God, I can't remember. Starts with an *A*—maybe it's *Angus,* Guardian of something…"

"I wasn't so old when Mom died. If I came by some

evening, could you tell me about her—I remember a lot of things, but maybe you know more. I'd like to hear—"

He stood, turning. "I have to go now." And then he went over the wall and was gone.

***

It seemed to me, the next day, that Patty Cake Pat was on his way up to Franz Junior's house, and he stopped by here the night before for a visit. And when he did get to them, the woman Madge was somehow aware of him. As to why he went there, I couldn't guess, but it made me curious.

The very next morning after the albino's brief visit, I could see the top of Franz's car going past my wall out to the paved road. Maybe he wanted a paper or some coffee or doughnuts. As soon as he was gone, my phone started ringing again, and, of course, it was Madge, and it was the same old story. This time, I did suggest that maybe she and Franz should get a dependable dog. When Franz got back, another phone call came immediately, and now he wanted to know what the hell I was thinking, wanting them to get a dog. An animal around their place? Who was supposed to take care of an animal, feed it, and clean up after it?

"Do you think we're going to go hunting, for Christ's sake?" he declared loudly on the phone, and then he hung up.

I have a few thoughts about the animals we hunt and use for hunting. Knowing how Jenny kept my picture, something in me that understood how clever an animal can be had awakened. I've been a hunter, and I know some animals are super smart, far smarter than we think. Even if we have the advantage over them, they seem to know how to double back or encircle their trails – and wait for us to make a mistake. All I know is that something in me was growling now when Franz was on the phone.

On one hunt, the only time I ever joined with a large party hunting in a country where there were still tigers, I was given some advice by an experienced person. He said he would never hunt a tiger even if he was given permission to do so. That was because once you were in the wilds where the tiger knew the terrain better than you did, there was the danger the tiger was hunting you more cleverly than you were hunting it. When we're hunted, maybe there's a tiger in each of us, and we just don't know it. Especially if it's a tigress protecting her cub.

***

If I anticipated I'd see Patty Cake Pat after another three or four weeks, I was wrong. Late the very next afternoon, Stinker began wagging his tail. I took my drink with me out onto the patio, and there he was, perched just about where he had been the previous night.

"How long did you know my mom? Did you know her when she was a little girl?"

He wanted to know everything I knew about her. He must have been around ten or eleven when she died. I wasn't sure. But he was young, so I decided to give him all I had in my heart and memory about Jenny. I couldn't remember not knowing her, for she and I started the elementary grades together. Even then, I wanted to protect her, because Jenny was so vulnerable and trusting. I knew she needed big lunky me. Right from the start, I had a crush on her, and in the middle grades, I became so possessive about her other boys kept away. I know people say your high school love won't be permanent, but she and I were serious about each other. We talked about marriage."

"So why didn't you get married, then?"

"Both our families said we should wait, to be sure. I respected her father a lot, and he said he knew a military life wouldn't be easy for Jenny, and he thought we should be really sure – so we followed all the advice. We would phone and write one another – and we'd let a year pass, and then we'd marry. So that's what we did. I gave her my class ring, but I made a mistake. I should have gotten her an engagement ring."

He was interested, leaning forward. It was time to be honest.

"I lost her. I stayed away too long. That's what I think. All of a sudden, I wasn't hearing much from her. I knew her father died, and that left her and her shy mother alone. I'm guessing the handsome son of a rich man swept her away from me."

"Money. Security and money."

"Franz thinks money does the trick, all right. He's offered me a cool thousand a month just to let him know when anyone—you, I guess—is approaching him. It must have worked for Jenny. When I got back, if she had been engaged, I could have won her back. But she was married already and pregnant."

"Pregnant with me."

"Yes. I was furious. Furious with myself for being away too long, and with her for not waiting for me. And she seemed different somehow, as if she wasn't quite the same Jenny I'd left. Anyway, I lost her."

He and I were both quiet for a few minutes, thinking.

"I trusted him when I was little," he finally said. "He told me I was going to be his lab assistant, going to be a scientist like him and my grandfather. Didn't turn out that way. Lies. One of the women he hired to school me, Mrs. Lightfoot, told me later on that he hated the sight of me when I was born, and he wanted to send me away from there, but my mom wouldn't agree because she loved me, and that made him mad."

I didn't tell him that when I attended a garden party, I saw his father and his girlfriend Madge smooching it up behind the house, and that is what made me decide to get the hell away from it all, to stay in the military after all. That was another mistake. I should have stuck around. I should have rescued her. If she had given me even the smallest hint she was in danger, I would have ripped her away from him.

I should have stuck with it right where I was and, later on, gone into that house and taken her out of there. But I didn't. I told him all that.

"Things don't always turn out right," he said. "Mrs. Lightfoot was so nice to me, she had a dog, and she brought him with her when she taught me. She let the dog sleep with me. Because sometimes I wasn't allowed to go back with my mom at night. And I surely wasn't allowed to have a dog."

He was over the wall and away, but I would see him again. Those first two occasions, I met him, were followed by others. What he said as he left this time stuck with me.

"Stinker's the dog I would have wanted, and you're the dad I should've had."

I was left wondering why he wasn't always allowed to be with his mom.

I didn't mention what I read in letters from friends – that Franz Junior had brought his mistress Madge into his home, right into the house where Jenny and his child were – giving her a title like social secretary or some such thing. She was pretty much running things, I was told.

After he left, I slept well that night. One of the things I told him was how beautiful Jenny was; and how I could remember her so well; how I could call up her image easily, standing before me confident and calm, gray eyes sparkling. Telling him that made an old wound close.

What needed questioning hadn't been approached: why was it that he was sneaking up on those two, bothering them so much? And how did he get here in the first place, for they certainly hadn't brought him along with them? I was going to have to ask about those things.

***

Most Friday afternoons, you can find Ted Davis and me at the local VFW. The fellows there aren't hard to please. They won't press their opinions on you. They just want peace for the country and sports on the bar TVs. They want to root for the underdog, and in each one of them, I suppose there's the desire to get back to their old unit. Good place to relax for lunch and a beer.

I met Ted long ago in Denver, Colorado, where he was with the police when I had to go to investigate a troublesome army offender. Ted's much younger than I am, and he's been retired longer than I have. When I finally retired and first walked into the VFW, it was a surprise to see Ted there. He, his wife Terri, and their daughter Misty are living just a few miles away from me.

Ted realized I have neighbors now in old Franz's house. I figure young Franz inherited that house after his father's death but just recently decided to move from Delaware to live in it.

There are lots of trails in the foothills and the heights beyond that house, and Ted and his family are fond of biking there. Sometimes they invite me to join them. Not me. I'm built for football, not a bike. Besides, some of those biking paths are game trails, and I figure a solitary biker like me would be an easy take-down for cougars. Ted always carries a weapon on his person, which is one reason he loves Arizona so much: a lot of people are packing pistols in this state. I'm sometimes one of them, but it takes some getting used to – so many people armed; how many threats possible.

Anyway, Ted noticed lights and signs of people there, and he remarked on it.

"Have you met your neighbors yet?" He was only mildly interested until he saw my reaction.

"Yeah, I know my neighbors. Known them for years. Not my favorite people."

Suddenly he was interested. So I told him about my dad and old Franz and about how I wasn't friends with young Franz and how he stole my girl away from me.

"And now the son is going up there to his place and scaring them. I guess that young man has reasons to be angry."

"A son? Scaring them?"

So I told him about that, too, about the son being an albino, all that. Ted was seriously quiet for a minute.

"You're sure he's not living with them, but he's around their place at night?"

"Not every night. Best I can tell, about once a month."

"Why?"

"Haven't found that out yet."

"But he's scaring them."

"Definitely. Security cameras installed, the whole bit."

"Pat, has it occurred to you the son is going to harm them, maybe kill them?"

"Nah. He hasn't got that in him. He's the victim here. He has his mother's eyes."

Ted was incredulous. "His mother's eyes! Has his mother's eyes! You know good and damn well the worst murderers of all, the most heartless, sadistic bastards, were victims first! That's how they got to be that murderous way, for Christ's sake! The meanest bastard I ever caught had an angel's face and big brown son-of-a-bitchin' eyes! Pat, the way they look has nothin' to do with it!" He was indignant.

"Then, since his looks aren't attractive, maybe the opposite is true. Looks bad doesn't mean a person is bad."

"But this is one that sounds bad, and maybe is bad. You said it yourself: he probably has reasons to be angry."

Then I remembered something that young man told me. He was allowed to go with Mrs. Lightfoot (she taught him math and science) into the backyard. He wasn't to appear in public or go to public school, but out back, where those huge generators were, he and she could walk. At a window above, the woman Madge appeared – Franz was behind her.

"You keep that monstrosity away from me," Madge called down to Mrs. Lightfoot.

"Does she mean me?" the boy asked.

"You're no monster. She is," came the reply.

I think of him now using my name. Patrick. He said he felt as if he and Mrs. Lightfoot were in a pit where a wild animal was kept – maybe a tiger – and someone was throwing stones down just to be mean. I had similar thoughts, and maybe that's why I recalled that.

"Maybe something is in all of us that could make us

killers," I said. "This is Friday, and they have hot dogs. You want a hot dog?"

"No, I don't want a goddamn hot dog!" Ted was spluttering. "I want to meet this Franz guy!"

"What you want to meet, really, is that gal Madge. She'll make you want to put her picture in the post office."

"You said this Franz took your gal away, and now here's the son – so where's his mother now? Where is she?"

"She committed suicide," I told Ted. "I think the son was still quite young then. I think loneliness and unhappiness killed her. Anyway, suicide was what I was told."

Ted was quiet, his eyes on me.

"In England," I said, "I saw a tombstone had on it just this: 'Here Lies The Unhappiest Man.' His family died of the plague. But he didn't. He died because he loved and missed them. I think of Jenny being cut off from the outside world and her son, with only my photograph to comfort her. And I cry, 'Murder! Murder! Most foul!'" I told Ted this; about how I felt.

"No chance the VFW will be hearing you yak it up about all this, right?"

"No. But I should get my gear ready. He could kill them and you and throw you in a ravine somewhere. Find out about what he's up to, Pat."

"He's not the only one with reasons to be angry," I said. "I've killed Franz Junior over and over in my mind. I might yet do that myself."

***

He showed up again several evenings later. I was sitting at my crude table out on the patio where I sometimes eat, cleaning my revolver. At first, he was perched on the garden wall again, but he asked if he could sit at the table where I was.

"If he comes down this road, maybe he can see me if I'm here," he said. "But I don't think he could if I was up higher, where you are."

"Come ahead, then," I said, knowing he meant Franz, of course.

When he settled across the table from me, I got my first really close look at him. I had asked myself if I had a son like him, could I have been a good parent? I believe I could have. Parents have children who are "different" all the time, and if anything, they love them even more. I thought about that since he told me his middle name was the same as mine. But seeing him up close was interesting, for his fingers were even longer than I estimated after seeing him at a distance, the eyes even larger, ears larger, too, and the nose so narrow. This Patrick was an illustration taken out of some book of Nordic myths.

"Is this your gun? What kind is it?" His long fingers touched the barrel.

"It's a Smith & Wesson .357 Magnum. Used a lot by the military."

"Are you a marksman with it?"

I thought of Ted, who once shot the weapon right out of the hand of a man who was holding hostages. From a considerable distance, he did that. Some men are born to be sharpshooters; I'm sure of that. I'm not one of them.

"No, I'm not. But I'm steady, and if I have to shoot, I know what to do."

His eyes were asking who I was going after.

"I'm awake early. Took the garbage can to the road, and I could smell some critter had been visiting us. Probably a wild cat. So it reminded me to take care of this."

He looked around.

"No, it was out front. I have some questions that need answers. How much do you hate your father? Do you want to kill him?"

The question made him blink and turn away from me a little.

"I know he caused my mother's death. I hold him accountable; and I hate him, but I wouldn't kill him."

"No? I've thought about it."

"If I did that, from then on, I'd run on emotion. Once we kill, we change course. Reason wouldn't be with me any more. Besides, I sort of blame myself. If I had been born perfect, then he might have been pleased. I think he might have."

"I should have stuck. I should have acted."

He gave a narrow-shouldered half shrug. "Regrets, regrets."

I holstered my weapon and folded it in a flannel cloth. I would put it under lock and key when I went into the house. Because I have no wife or children, I don't have to be as careful, but I have reservations about a gun in the house. I think it's a good thing to have, just as long as you remember that children will find a weapon no matter where you hide it. Lock it up. Period. And I seldom carry.

"All right. Let's not kill him. Next question is this: you go up there to his place, and you're causing them grief somehow or other. So what are you doing and why, and how did you get here, anyway? You sure didn't come with them."

"That's more than one question."

"Just tell me."

"That takes a lot of telling. And you won't like it, either."

"And while you're at it, explain that part about how you didn't get to sleep where your mother was. You had to sleep somewhere else."

***

Ted had told somebody about our conversation. I could tell. It seemed to me there were some people staring at me when I came into the VFW. He swore he hadn't, except for telling Terri and his daughter Misty.

"That's it, then. If you tell a couple of women, you've told the world."

"No, no, not Terri and Misty."

"And Misty isn't even your daughter's name."

Her name is Mildred, after a favorite aunt, but she doesn't like that name, so she improvised Misty from Mildred and said close enough. I was in a bad mood because it was blazing hot outside, and there was a wind that was carrying dust and pollen all over the place.

Ted says he understands my distrust of women now that he knows about Jenny's death.

"Hard to trust again. You've been more loyal to a dead woman than I've been to a living one." He was unfaithful to his wife just once and was so guilt-stricken about it he never strayed again.

"If Terri knew I talked about this, she'd kill me. She doesn't know." In fact, he shies away from any attractive women he comes in contact with.

Not stupid me, though. I always get attracted and involved, like a damn fool. But at some point, when a relationship gets too comfortable and nice, I back off. I've lost count of how many times that happened. Sometimes the hurt female's feelings lead to unfortunate things she says to her friends, and whoever else will listen: oh, he tried to push me around; oh, he's so bossy; oh, I think he's a homosexual. Everything that means it's not her fault he's not committing.

"Terri says you've been walking with Carol," Ted tells me.

"You two know the Bentleys?"

Now Ted's looking at me thoughtfully.

"What do you mean 'the Bentleys'?"

"Carol and her husband, of course."

Ted's studying my face.

"Pat, Carol's husband's been dead for years."

Son of a bitch. That's what a female says to you – mentions husband – when she wants you to lay off, when she has no interest in you whatsoever. That's what you say to an old man, too old for you. To Patrick Monahan, the man women have been chasing all this time. By God, that's news.

"Well, let's have a beer. It's hot out there, and we have to brave it sooner or later."

"Yes, and he doesn't have murder on his mind. Definitely not."

So then I tell him how this Patrick was treated when he was a little kid, that son of Franz Gephardt Junior. I had been putting it off because it sounds strange.

"He used his little son like a lab rat or a monkey, Ted. For years. For as long as a week at a time every month. It had to do with low frequency radio waves. They'd do this at night, because during the day there would be people who were supposed to educate the boy, and those people were told he was sick and so they needn't come in for the week. They'd be called if he got better. That's the lie they were told.

"It wasn't just simple experiments. It was a government project, something for the defense department. He told me sometimes there would be people who looked very official coming in at night to look at him. There were also a few people Patrick thought were medical workers."

Ted was disbelieving.

"What was it about, for God's sake, if it's true?"

"His middle name is my name, Patrick, so I'm calling him that. Patrick says it was to see what the effects would be on human beings when they got hit by low frequency radio waves. He says they would start off easy on him the first night, but each night it got stronger and longer. It made him submissive and groggy, and he'd do whatever he was told. It made him have awful headaches when it was too strong, and joint aches. It affected his eyesight. Hearing, too."

"Why did they do all that for, anyway? What purpose?"

"This is how Patrick explained it to me. You got a bunch of people planning an attack. They get hit by low frequency radio waves. They don't even know they're getting it. All of a sudden, they're disoriented. They can't even remember what they met for. You can wipe out their purpose and maybe replace it with some other thing. Patrick says he only figured out when he was getting hit because sometimes he heard a clicking noise, and sometimes it was a funny kind of fizzing noise he heard. At the end of the week, Franz would wrap his head in a tea towel dipped in ice water to help him with the pain. Sometimes it made him cry. Patrick says when Mrs. Lightfoot got into an argument with Franz, she was told it was called a behavior modification program."

"Couldn't somebody stop that? For God's sake, those people knew better."

"Patrick told me his father convinced him he was helping his country and if he would stick with it, he would be a scientist, too, like his father and his grandfather. Once his grandfather left for Arizona, when the boy was so young, who was going to stop Franz Junior? I don't think his grandfather even knew what was happening. People in the neighborhood and the community probably thought the boy was being educated privately and being well cared for. That's my guess. He was told that he would get to see his mother the following weekend if he was a good test subject. That happened to him once a month, every month for years. I'm surprised he survived it. I bet his father hoped he wouldn't."

***

Sometimes we have to deal with nations that aren't like us, and that's hard. For example, if you're some nation out in the Far East, and you're in such a hard place your people have to eat dogs, nobody is going to fault you for that. But if you like to torture those dogs before you kill them because you think that makes their meat taste better, that makes you something sub-human. And if somebody like me is sent into your country, it's hard for your people not to see my scorn. That's what makes it hard for me to have Franz Junior as a neighbor. He was torturing that child and that mother.

Patrick told me Jenny was spoken to with so much ridicule and so many insults by Madge that she tried to hide away in just a few rooms so the household staff wouldn't witness her being so humiliated. What kind of father and husband does such things? What kind of defense department knows of such experiments and does nothing?

I still have lots of questions. Ted wants everything explained at once.

"You're a very... big... slow... person, Pat. You still don't know anything."

***

I had fixed a sandwich and was eating it at that patio table, the next time Patrick came over the wall.

The edge of night here is nice. That's when people choose to walk or sit on their patios. The temperature drops twenty degrees or more, away from the heat of the day. Stinker had been napping but now settled near our visitor. Like Ted, I wanted to know how this fellow survived, how he got here in the first place, and more, but I knew it would unfold when he, Patrick, wanted it to.

"Do you want that pickle?" he asked.

"You can have it. You can go in the kitchen and make a sandwich if you're hungry."

For a while, there were only kitchen noises and eating, though all the while he was looking at me, inspecting me. I have my father's blue eyes and some ancestor's staggering height, but I'm certainly not as heroic as I look.

"Were you ever in battle?" he asked. The military part of me. Of course, that.

"No, I wasn't. I was close to battle lines, though. My job was to find people and question them. Sometimes, I was to bring them in and have them questioned by others if it was our own military."

"You were acting alone?"

"Oh, no. I had lots of help. Translators when I needed them.

Plenty of help. Nothing heroic. I was around people who were heroes, though."

"You want to ask more questions about me, then?"

"Yes, for one thing, do you still suffer any effects from what you experienced?"

"I don't think so. I think after I went through one week, I'd be wobbly and not all there, but the second week, I'd still be getting better, and the third week, I'd be normal, but I'd be dreading the next week. I'd bounce back. There were chemical changes in my brain, though; I'm sure of that. I don't think my father realized that the person who endured the experiments would understand its outcomes and the consequences better than he did. I had the lab and the library of my grandfather. I came to understand everything he wrote about in his journals. I was amazed I could understand what he wrote."

Stinker got a piece of ham under the table. I don't do that, but so what. No wonder Stinker liked this young man.

"After Mom's death, I told Mrs. Lightfoot about what was happening. She had a terrible argument with my father. He told her she might just disappear if she didn't look out. That it was an important project, but it was about to end anyway, and he wasn't going to let her quit because he wanted to keep his eye on her. She was to keep her mouth shut. I think he scared her.

"She's the one who told me it was called a behavioral modification program. Here's the thing now, see ... this is what I found out about myself. I don't need the equipment to generate radio pulse waves. I can do it all by myself. I AM the equipment." He tapped his forehead. His eyes were twinkling with some sort of excitement about himself.

"Pretty soon, my father and Madge were gone a lot, and I had the run of the library. I read everything and organized it, and I put journals into a trunk while they were off having a grand old life. He's found out how to live like a rich man. Which he is. I'll give him that.

"I should go now. Do things early. I hope I can stop by next week and talk some more. Stinker, you be a good boy, now." And he went over the wall.

The next day, I heard Madge and Franz at it again, arguing. It began to dawn on me that after I suspected he'd been at them again, they deteriorated into something awful, and they didn't seem to care if I heard them.

***

So now I'm aware that Patrick (the younger Patrick, the one who thinks I should have been his father) is sure that after the experiments he went through, he got to be super smart. Smart enough that all his grandfather wrote is clear to him. And what is also clear is that I'm not anywhere near as smart as he is.

***

So, okay, I've had a few drinks.

I'm with Ted at the VFW, and it's even hotter than the day before, and there are fires in the northern part of the state, and even in the southern part where I didn't think there was anything growing there that could burn.

By then, Patty Cake Patrick had visited me once more.

"Have you made any progress finding out stuff?" Ted asked. I knew he wanted, as I did, to find out what this young Patrick was doing to Franz Junior and his mistress.

"Sort of ... and no. It takes time."

Ted frowned. "You're impossible," he said.

"He's quit whinin' and started in testifyin' about himself," I said. "His face lights up when he's talkin' now. He says he can make his own electricity—"

"What?"

"Yep. Can do that. He says he can. He says I probably could do that, too. He thinks I've got about 100 watts in me. Then he laughs. Ha Ha."

Ted is staring at me.

"He says low frequency radio waves happen all by themselves in nature. *Or* they can be manufactured. And he can do that. He can produce those low frequency waves all by himself. He doesn't need any big old generator or anything else. He says from his mind he can do that. No wall can stop him. And if he's outside your house and you're inside, he can find you in there just by using his mind because you generate heat."

"Pat, have you been drinking?"

"He *says* UFOs are probably interested in us because of our progress with weaponry. I said to him the UFOs are probably interested in us because we taste like bacon. Then he stared at me like you're staring, and he laughed and said I'm a very strange person."

Ted was choking on his beer. What I didn't say was that now Patrick and Stinker would sit beside each other on the sofa and watch TV. And Patrick wants to bring a small trunk full of his grandfather's journals and ledgers and papers and keep that here at my house. For safe keeping.

"Has he done anything that proves he can do all this stuff?"

"Nope."

"Let me come over there and shake the stuffin's out of him."

"Jenny's boy. No shakin' stuffin's."

Then Terri comes in and joins us.

"Hi," she says. "You seeing Carol now?"

That's another sour disappointing thing. "No," I say. "I haven't seen her lately. She's busy. Probably."

"Pat here might not have it all together for Carol," Ted said and grinned.

"Ted, you talk too much," Terri said to him.

So this has been a horrible day.

Later, on my way back to my home, I think back to the British woman I was in contact with when I was on assignment in Indonesia. She reminded me of Jenny. She gave great parties at her quarters where everybody who was anybody gathered. I was younger then, and I'm guessing I looked pretty good in dress uniform. She said so, anyway ... and she loved to dance ... and yes, I did go to bed with her, and more than once. She visited Great Britain now and then. She wanted me to go with her on that next excursion to Somerset.

"Don't you want to see how you fit in with the landed gentry?"

Smiling, she said that as she tugged at my arm and my heart.

I already knew how I would fit in with the landed gentry. I wouldn't. Wherever I go, it's like I have a sign on me that says, "Dumbo American and can't change."

It could have been a turning point for me. I could have gone with her. I told her the truth that I was on assignment, but if I'd asked for the time, I'd have gotten it. I could have married that dear woman and lived happily with her and our children... and maybe now I'd be sitting pretty in some nice old manor house, hoping my sheep and my barley crop were okay.

Instead, I was going to my house where I would deal with some super intelligent man who was turning into kind of an electric eel ... who would get all excited someday and set himself and my place on fire.

I was curious enough that I contacted the daughter of a woman I knew once, long ago. The daughter was, like her mom, also in intelligence. I asked her to find out if, way back when, there had ever been any project by defense about low frequency radio waves and their effect on human beings, or anything called behavior modification. She found something. It was called Project Waves. She thought it must have had something to do with the navy. It looked as if it was done and over with and shelved away, but it still had its top-secret classification.

So I certainly wasn't any smarter than when I started out. Especially when Patrick pointed out that animals use radio waves.

"Elephants use radio frequency to communicate..." he began.

Then he looked at me. "You don't know anything at all, do you?" And he looked so mournful when he said that. This was going to take some getting used to.

***

Drinking doesn't help. Obviously.

A few days later, when I returned from the grocery store, I could hear the TV in front of the house was on. I knew he was there with Stinker. He's taken to calling me "Big Patrick", so I guess he's "Little Patrick". Anyway, his grandfather's trunk was there, open, and it wasn't such a big deal as I'd feared. It was a small thing, but very full of ledgers and journals and loose pages, all looking as if they were hand written. He was on the sofa with several pages of his grandfather's, and he looked excited as if what he was reading was pretty important.

"I understand this," he said. "This can be done."

I wasn't in the mood to hear about that. What I wanted to know was all that other stuff. How he got here ... matter of fact, how that trunk got here, and what he was doing to Franz and why, and how he managed to live, about money and such... all that. So I was blunt. I headed for the patio. Getting anything for supper could wait.

"You come with me," I said. "We need to talk. And you know I want to know what it's all about between you and him up the road there."

He did follow me, but he was protesting all the way. "No, you won't like me. It. You won't like It. What I just read... it's important, really. You'll know how much when I tell you about it."

That seemed to bother him. He said, as if it was an afterthought, "What do you know about radio waves?"

All right. Time to be honest. "Nothing."

"Well, it's got a lot to do with civilized countries. Think TV and the remote, microwaves – and that's a lot more than just for cooking –and submarines – because the low frequency waves travel so well in salt water –" He paused to reflect, across from me at the patio table. "Uh... satellites and cell phones and GPS... uh... your car ignition and computers and the way the police and fire departments communicate... well, just think *power grids*. Because that's what it is, really. It's *power grids* and all forms of communications... except maybe smoke signals.

"See, it's like this. It's electric and magnetic moving

together at the speed of light ... well, at the speed of light if it was in a vacuum, but forget that. See, it moves in *pulses*. It moves in *waves*. Or *cycles*. One name it's called is a *Megahertz* ..." And now he was glancing at me to see if I was paying attention. "That's one million cycles per second. And it can be even faster. Faster it goes, higher the frequency gets and the more heat it gives off. It's straight but bends, too, so it can reach way beyond the horizon to far places all over...

"I've tried to tell you, animals can use it, like elephants... when you're talking communication, that's what it is. Even plants—"

"You can talk to plants?" I ventured.

"Not with words, actually. It's like in the Bible when Jesus got mad at a fig tree and the fig tree died. Plants are aware... well, let's see..." He got up from the table and moved to the rambler rose bush where it had command of the back wall. "It's like this," he said. It seemed to me he bent his head toward that rose bush a little, and maybe he moved his hand a little. No matter. I saw what happened next. I saw one long, green branch of that rambler rise and lift itself up off the top of the wall. It sort of trembled, sort of shook itself, like something going *BRRRRrrr*. And then it went slowly back into its original position. I think it was that last part, how it knew how to get back to where it came from that horrified me more than anything else.

I was open-mouthed, stupefied. He, on the other hand, was prattling along as if nothing unusual happened.

"...senses things, doesn't know words... well, I don't think so, anyway, but some pets do know words... they can even anticipate your thoughts... share your feelings."

He came back to the table. I was kind of fearful the rose

bush might follow him.

"Oh, oh, oh! About those pages. This is important," he said. "My grandfather thought the inventions about low frequency radio waves were the most important inventions of our century. And he thought more inventions would even change how wars are fought in years to come. Here's what he thought could be coming. See, if electromagnetic pulse could be incorporated in artillery shells, why, that could attack radio frequency networks, and that's what *everything* uses. So such an attack could knock out the power grids for the whole area. Even worse, if a nuclear explosion included it, if that explosion happened up high over a highly populated area of any nation, you could knock out the power grid for almost all the whole nation. And you know what? I understand this. It could be done. I could do that. I know I could."

I had the feeling I was going to hear, "My grandfather says", a lot from here on in. Even as he left, he was saying his grandfather said in those notes the only defense where behavior modification was concerned would be to have robots with their own intelligence. "He says they wouldn't be affected." I don't know if I can last through a whole lot more. This is going to take some getting used to.

***

It wasn't long before the phone rang, and it was Madge again. She was alone and frightened. She was sure there was somebody around who wanted to harm her. She was certain earlier she could sense that intruder's presence, and Franz wasn't around. He was in Delaware again. I was in no mood to deal with Madge. I suggested she needed to go into town and stay at a motel till he got back. And while she was there, she should see what she could do about getting some people to stay there at the house with her... well, no... not in the house, but let's say they had a trailer right next to the house—that would be ideal, and that's what she should do. She seemed to brighten up a little at that. After I hung up, I was exhausted. I was too scared of my rose bush to go out on the patio. I put that little trunk behind the sofa and covered it with one of my mom's table runners. I took the pages little Patrick had left on the sofa and put them on the side table beside the sofa, with an ashtray on top to hold them down – and then just went to sleep on the sofa.

***

I wasn't very presentable the next morning. My shirt was rumpled, but it was an old shirt anyway, one pocket half off. I had on old work pants, and I smelled like manure. I'd slept on the sofa, and I looked like it. I didn't even bother with brushing my hair or my teeth. I just went outside to finish up fertilizing the roses with the last of that manure. I'd started yesterday. Now it was early morning. Who's going to see me?

I couldn't bring myself to get close to that rambling rose. I threw some fertilizer at the base of the plant.

"I hate you!" I exclaimed to it. "You scared me to death! I'm not even going to get close to you!"

Immediately, a voice rose from the service road behind the wall. "Are you talking to me, Pat?" it said.

The voice was familiar. I edged closer to the wall, and there was Carol Bentley standing in the road, her eyes wide, questioning.

Good women change as they grow older, but I think their eyes are somehow always and forever the same wide, inquisitive eyes they had as a child. Those eyes were fastened on me now, and what a sight they were seeing. A wreck of an old man.

"No, no... not. I was talking to this rose bush."

The eyes got even bigger and rounder.

"Well, it has prickles and brambles and thorns and such."

"Yes, it does." And she nodded, smiling a little.

"Where have you been, anyway? I haven't seen you lately."

She told me her mother was sick, so she went to her to help. It was when I said I hoped her mother was better I saw her trembling. She had just come back from her mother's funeral. Tears flowed.

I knew because I'd asked Terri and Ted—here was a woman whose husband died, and whose father was also gone. Now the mother was dead. There were no children. What I was seeing in her face and her eyes was the fear she just couldn't find it within herself to go forward bravely any more.

Had Jenny looked out of a window seeking rescue and seeing no reason to go on?

There was a gate at the back of the garden that opened onto the service road.

"You stay right there, Carol," I said. "I'm coming to get you."

For the next hour or so, we sat at that patio table and talked about our families. About good times and bad. How lucky we were to have had such parents, such good times. We drank sweet iced tea. She even laughed a little. I walked her to her house nearby, and I told her she had friends, and I was one of them and that I would come to help her no matter how late or early it might be.

Good women never should be allowed to despair.

There was a poem my mom quoted now and then. It was a very short poem, and I'm sorry I can't remember those few lines of it. It compared death to some old door set in a garden wall. Once we get through it, I said to Carol; I expect we marvel at how silly all our fears were.

I walked back home humming to myself, mentally, "You've got a Friend in me."

There's my own image about death, something that's conjured up to comfort me ahead of time, even before I think of being afraid of anything. My dad had his old desk with those phones and those phone numbers on it … and all that's still there in my bedroom.

"If you're ever in a tough spot," he said, half joking, "you just use any of these numbers to get through to the *Cabrel* and tell them to get in touch with me. I'll come get you. I'll find out the next port of call for the *Cabrel*, and I'll get you and me on board her, and we'll be safe."

So that's what I would want to have death be for me, if I get any say about it. I told Patrick about that when he saw Dad's stuff on that table. He sat down and got some paper out from the drawer, and copied the numbers. I asked about that, and he said he would like to go aboard that freighter with me.

"All right, then. I'll come get you out of a jam. Unless you're in jail." It was said in a joking manner, but he put those numbers in his pocket, I noticed.

***

Now at the VFW, Ted had enlisted Win (Winfred) to plead with me about Patrick.

"You said you wouldn't talk about this," I said. "Next it'll be Win's pal and on and on."

"You need help," they protested. "You could be in danger. He's not telling you anything."

"You've got to find out what he's all about, Pat," they agreed.

"He's probably a damn drug runner," one suggested.

"He's ashamed of something. It'll come out, I'm sure of it," I said.

They groaned.

Then I remembered something that made me feel much better. She called me, "Pat."

***

I'm not liking the war games Patty Cake Patrick has discovered. He probably thinks playing shoot 'em up makes him a military fellow, but I don't care much for that. Stinker sits there beside him and seems to be paying attention to what's going on, which amazes me, for that dog never watches television.

I get their attention by turning it off. "We have to talk," I say firmly, "about Madge. Because she's driving me nuts. She calls on the phone, or she turns up at the door. She always senses when you're around, Patrick. One time she was complaining that she just knew that intruder was around somewhere, and her intruder was sitting just a room away from me. Has she seen you?"

Patrick answered thoughtfully. "Yes, I wasn't careful one time when I was walking around their place, and I blundered into them. She saw me, I'm sure of that. She screamed."

"And now? Can she sense you when you're nearby?"

"Maybe. Some people are more sensitive than others."

"Do you hate her?"

"Sorry to say I do."

"Enough to want to kill her?"

"No, no."

"Patrick, then do you feel hostile toward anyone else, besides her?"

"No… but I did cause a man's car to quit on him. He was rude."

"What?"

"He cut me off, cut right in front of me, gave me the finger."

"You could have caused an accident?"

"No, I stayed right behind him, all the way, when he drifted off onto the shoulder."

"Wait a minute… you have a car, Patrick?"

"Sure. It's a nice car. I have a driver's license, all that."

"Where are you getting the money for that? You have no high school diploma, no skills, no… are you a drug runner or something like that?"

"No, of course not!" He was indignant. His gaze fell downward. This was Jenny's son, and I saw a lot of Jenny in him. He wanted me to like him; I could see that. I decided to avoid this part of him for a while.

"All right, all right. Later on for that. But I don't have a clue about all of what you can or can't do. What if you were in a plane or on a boat and a missile was coming? Could you destroy the missile?"

"I don't think so. No. But if it was a missile sitting on its pad and it was about to take off, I could stop it. I'm sure of that, even though I haven't done that ever. And I know I could mess up submarines. Sure I could do that."

"Could you burn somebody up?"

"No! For God's sakes, you're harping on the wrong things here! Has it ever occurred to you that I might not be the only one can do stuff? What if there's somebody can really make volcanoes get active, things like that? It's what we do to Nature makes me get mad. To the trees, for example."

"Trees? Trees, now?"

"Majestic oaks, for one thing. Ancient priests believed they could get questions answered by the way they could get an oak to move its leaves. Did you know that?"

He turned his body toward me, obviously passionate about oak trees. "Britain chopped down almost all their tallest oaks for their navy, for the masts and cross beams of their ships. Here, on the Chesapeake Bay, they did the same thing with the islands in the Bay. They stripped the Bay's islands of the strongest trees. And when the big trees were gone, the wind and water won every winter. Whole islands disappeared. It was like murder."

He relaxed, patting Stinker.

"Could you get in touch with some of those coyotes out in the hills?"

He shrugged. "I suppose. But you never hear of much good coming from those guys." He seemed to me to be looking at the phone.

"You worry too much about what I can do. Maybe you need to hear from a friend. I can sweep your mind—"

The phone on the side table rang. It was an old-style phone that had been sitting there for years. I didn't know it could work. I always used and answered the newer phone in the kitchen. But never mind. It rang, and I answered it.

There was some static, but I could hear him, and it was Ted. He just got the urge to call me. He said he wanted to be sure everything was all right. Sure it was, I told him. Everything is fine here. The whole time, I was looking at Patrick.

After I hung up, he smiled, sort of like he was saying, "See?"

I hadn't learned much... a little bit, I guessed.

"I don't even know how or where you live," I said.

"Since I'm here now, I've had to rent a little house."

When he saw my mouth fly wide open at that news, he got flustered.

"It gets hot here! I have to have air conditioning!"

At least for now, I give up.

***

I'm sorry I ever gave my phone number to Franz Junior and Madge. Whenever I am feeling good, perhaps when I'm on the patio just relaxing, that phone in the kitchen will ring, and off we go again.

This time it was Franz. Being his usual nasty self.

"Now you've got Madge putting that couple in their trailer right up my ass! Can't even flush the toilet they don't hear it! And they're using our electricity! Dumbass idea! That's no help! She's worse than ever with her danger, danger yammering! Those damn cameras aren't working right! They're crap, and so are you! This is what I'm paying you every month for?"

Then slam/click, end of phone call.

I was left pondering on that last bit. I smoked my cigar and let a new suspicion come into my little mind. I was still chewing on that when I saw Patrick again the following week.

"My, my," I said. "Franz called me up complaining about how he's paying me and how he's not getting his money's worth. You know anything about that?"

"Oh," he said. He was suddenly looking at the floor.

Maybe he could tell the time to own up had arrived. He sort of drew himself together and launched his confession. It was going to be a long evening.

"Yes, well, he does think he's paying you. But actually, it's a check made out to me. He only thinks it's paying you. He's paying me. You did say you didn't want him to pay you any money. So I decided he could pay me instead of you."

"And just how does that work? How do you get it, in the mail?"

"Oh, no. He makes out a check, and he puts it in your mailbox the first of the month when it's dark, and he's thinking you get it during the night or early in the morning. Actually, I get it. I know, that's weird, but that's his... well, the way he does things."

"A thousand dollars, that's what you're getting?"

"Oh, no, much more than that. It's seven thousand a month. Paid first of every month."

"Jesus Lord Christ, Patrick! You're robbing the man! Jail time!"

"Not going to happen. And he's very wealthy, won't even miss it. Besides, I didn't have any choice. On yours, maybe I had a choice, but not with it at first."

"Oh, yeah, you had a choice. Sure you did, and do—"

"No, not really. You're not going to listen, I can tell. If only you would listen, you'd understand."

"All right, dammit. Listening."

"All the people who were helping me were gone. Mrs. Lightfoot was the last one, and she gave me her phone number and address before she left. Just me and the staff were there in the house. One chef told me my father and Madge were traveling in Central America, but they'd be back. When they did get back, one of the first things he did was tell me my usefulness was over, and he wanted me to get out of the house."

Well, that was a shocker.

"About old were you, then, Patrick?"

"I was a little over fifteen. And I was terrified. I'd never been out and about in the world, and I had no place to go. He said I could take whatever I wanted, but I had to get out. And never come back, not in the daytime, anyway. The first of each month, he would put a check for $1,000, made out to me, in his mailbox at dusk, and during the night, I was to come get it. He would give me that much and not a penny more. As to where I could go, he didn't care. That was my problem."

I tried to imagine how I would have handled it if I had been told to shove off when I was fifteen years old. I couldn't. My parents loved me.

"I took what was left of my mom's stuff, and the trunk with all my grandfather's papers, and all my clothes and papers and stuff, like my birth certificate – and before I left, I called Mrs. Lightfoot, and I begged her to come get me. She did; God bless her. I'm forever grateful to her and her children."

"You want some iced tea?" I could tell this was going to take a while, and it's been my experience that everything is better with iced sweet tea.

"Yeah, that would be nice." So, there was a break for getting some tea for both of us. He sat down at the patio table.

"How long did you stay with them?"

"Almost five years. She didn't have much, so I just cashed that check each month and turned the money over to her. There were two daughters struggling to get through college. I didn't see them much. But when I did, they were very nice. Nobody seemed to resent my being there, one more mouth to feed. There was a grown son, Paul, who had a responsible job, and he was the main financial support for them. I got to know him pretty well, and we got along as if I was a relative. He taught me how to play chess. I like that family. I'm still in touch with Paul and Mrs. Lightfoot."

"Why'd you leave?"

"Yes, getting to that. I could see how tough things were, and her car was old and getting ready to die on them, so I knew what I had to do."

Oh, my. Here we go, I was thinking.

"At night, I went back to the estate house. All I had to do was stand outside. There was a security guy who had his rooms on the first floor, and I could sense him there, and there was someone in the kitchen. My father and Madge, I picked up on the third floor together. I sent low frequency waves on them repeatedly until they were completely submissive. I instructed him to make the monthly checks out for $7,000 each time. What's more, he was instructed to call the corporation lawyer he knew best and inform him that the bank was to honor all such checks because he was making those checks out to support his son. And in corporation meetings, he would speak of it with that specific lawyer to confirm his decision to issue such checks. I didn't figure he would even glance at bank statements – and I was aware of those – but the bank might call to check on it with him, so it had to be taken care of. He would continue to speak of the checks as if they were for $7,000, but he would always think of them as being for $1,000 each month, and he would see a seven as if it were a one.

"And that worked nicely. For the longest time, I gave Paul $4,000 a month, and I kept back $3,000 for myself. The problem is that when you make people do that kind of stuff, they don't remember what they did, not at all, but they know something isn't right. I speak about this because I went through it so often. For weeks, they will be out of sorts, and just when they get back to normal, here I come again, near the first of the next month, to emphasize the instructions again. Or maybe add to or change stuff. It can tear behavior apart. I didn't have much sympathy for them. But yeah, it must have been hard on them. Whatever had been done to me, now I was putting it on them. Rich, huh?"

"So, again... why'd you leave there?"

"Guess they decided they needed a change. House went up for sale, and Paul went there as if there was a bill due, demanding to know where he could send the bill for what was owed. The staff finally gave him an address when he threatened to sue them. My father and Madge were already in Arizona. There would be no more money coming from them unless I could get to them, so I came here. Once I looked the situation over, I saw the same thing would work here just as it had up in Delaware, so I just continued it. He leaves his check for $7,000 in his mailbox the first of each month. His mailbox is right here at the edge of the paved road, and I get the check during the night. It's lovely. It hasn't improved their love life, but they never got along that well anyway."

I was puffing away on my cigar. I'm not the brightest man, but Franz has his mailbox pretty close to mine. Mine is out there on that paved road, too. There's an old beat-up mailbox attached to the house next to one of those French doors, but it's all rusted out. I should remove the thing, and I will, one of these days ... but it's the mailbox on the road that I use. The one attached to the house hasn't got any bottom in it at all.

"Now, wait, Patrick. You did say he puts the check he thinks he's paying to me in *my* mailbox? Is that right?"

"Yep. I get the check for $7,000 he thinks is $1,000 for me out of that mailbox of his, and then I go to your mailbox and get the $7,000 check he's thinking is $1000 for you when it's $7,000 for me."

"That's $14,000 a month you're getting from him!"

I'm thunderstruck. This fellow is into major crime.

"Well, the last took some doing, I must admit. But I instructed him to contact that one lawyer he knows best again. And that corporate lawyer has contacted the bank and told them the additional $7,000 made out to me each month is for my education, my college, and to help with living costs. That works nicely. And I reinforce it every time I hit on them. Before the first of the month, every time."

I guess he can see from my face what I think about this.

"I send Paul $4,000, as usual, every month, and I add quite a bit more, too, each month. When he adds that to his salary, they're doing just fine. And I don't think I had much of a choice about that. Who could live on $1000 a month? I would have starved or frozen to death if not for Mrs. Lightfoot. My father meant for me to die. I think so, anyway."

I was sitting in silence, chewing on my cigar. Maybe I was wishing I could talk with Jenny, or somebody like her, for a little advice.

And there was a bit more.

"I will admit, when you mentioned how he offered you that money every month, something inside me said, *Hey! Here's a chance for even more!* I admit that. Yeah, I thought like a robber when I realized that. You remember when a judge asked the bank robber – was it Dillinger? – 'Why do you rob banks?' and the bank robber said, 'Because that's where the money is.' I was thinking just like that bank robber."

***

I'm beginning to realize why it is some older male family members sit in stony silence. They have no idea what to do. Anything they can think of could be wrong.

If the couple being plundered were some dear sweet sort, and the person doing them harm was some punk, I'd want him to be thrown in jail. But young Patrick has been doing for himself what a loving parent should have been doing for him: supporting him, providing money for what should be his education, all that good stuff. It's just that the way he's doing it could put him in jail.

I believe Dad would have been telling me to apply common sense. So I'm sitting tight and keeping quiet except for telling a couple of people about it. I've told Carol about Patrick, leaving some things out... well, leaving a lot out... and I've told Ted pretty much everything. It's left Ted aghast, but he's sharing my opinion that keeping still on all this is the best thing to do. I don't want Patrick in jail.

Patrick needs to be cautioned, though. People who can do unusual things get to be talked about. That's the last thing he needs to have happen. He needs to keep a low profile. There are a couple of dangers: one is that some foreign government might take him off and make him do Lord knows what against his own country. The second thing that has crossed my mind is even worse – his own country might find him to be an embarrassment and throw him in jail. Then everybody's happy, except him, of course.

He's promised me he'll try to be no problem. "You could go to jail, too, couldn't you? For not turning me in soon as you knew about all I do?"

That thought has crossed my mind.

"The next time you manipulate his thinking, you should make Franz contact that corporate lawyer he knows so well one more time. Have him tell that lawyer that all taxes on money he's given you should be paid by Franz himself and not by you—that should be done because you don't have any job or business, and so Franz must do it for you. The lawyer should take care of the IRS."

He smiled. "I didn't think of that," he said. "It's good you thought of it. You're beginning to think like I do."

That is the most frightening thing anybody's said to me lately.

***

Carol and I walked the dogs this evening. It was cool, and the stars were appearing overhead. The temperature really drops here when the sun goes down.

We'd talked about Jenny and Patrick, and now Carol said she hoped young Patrick could someday lead a normal life and be just another citizen. I don't see how.

At her house, we stopped. I'd say goodbye there and then would continue on down the street to my place.

"I hope you won't mind if I give you a hug," she said. That's what she did, not letting me say yes or no—not that I would have said no because I wouldn't have.

"You're a good guy. Don't you worry too much," she whispered. Then she kissed my ear. When she did that, my whole body sprang to life.

I went home smiling. Maybe I'm not as old as I thought.

***

It's a good thing I have a cigar to puff on and chew on because young Pat's constant quoting his grandfather gets on my nerves so much. Old Franz was a staunch conservative, a republican, and my dad was, like all us Monahans, a devoted democrat. How the two of them were friends is beyond me, but they were. Now I had to be patient and listen to Patrick ranting on and on about all the doomsday stuff his grandfather believed.

"My grandfather thought," he says, "that the United States is on its way out. That it's all divided against itself, weakening itself, and that invaders will make quick work of us all—" until finally I have to speak up.

"Could you tone it down a little about what your grandfather said about things? I know I'm not as smart as you or your father or your grandfather, but I'm one of the men who might not agree with that."

"But how could you possibly not agree? It's like the fall of Rome all over again… I mean, Rome weakened after centuries of firm, wise law."

"Then," I said, "if we go down, at least let us go down fighting for the right things. Not divided, but letting steadfast men pull things together. When you're in a tight place,

Patrick—and I've been that way a couple of times—you don't care about the race or the religion or the politics of the men who're there with you. You know they'll drag you away from your enemies if you're wounded or dead. You know they'll stick with the fighting and not run away. You know all that because every one of them has these three invisible white feathers of honesty, honor and courage. Those are stuck on their caps and in their minds."

These were things I wanted him to know, maybe before it was too late if even half of what his grandfather said was true.

Patrick was looking at a newspaper, sitting there, but I knew he was listening, even if he wasn't looking at me.

"Yes, I know how deeply we're divided. Some people hating anybody who's black, somebody else hating anybody who's white, but at least all those citizens have their skins intact. You're sweating it because of the color of your skin. That's a problem, but it's minor when you consider I can think of at least three men who would change places with you in a minute. One of them lost both legs, and one has half his face left. But they're steadfast men, and most of them would go again if they had to, to fight again."

"Did you ever marry anybody?" he asked softly.

"No. I came close to it with one woman. But I couldn't get over losing your mother."

He looked at me.

"You're rugged looking and tall. You can imagine how it is when somebody like me shows up for a job interview. All of a sudden, that job was filled just this morning. Too bad. Let's face it. I'm the troll who crawled out from under the bridge."

His eyes were heartbreaking. There was Jenny in them, saying *save my son, save my son, save my son.*

I put the cigar into the ashtray. Damned thing was out anyway.

"I'll tell you what you do. You find a talented tailor. He makes you a snappy dresser, and you wear a snappy hat, too. You say to anybody you deal with, no matter what your job is or what your business is, 'I'm sorry everybody can't be as good looking and as cool as I am, but there's more to me than just looks. I'm the man you can depend on.' And you accept the fact that privately people will say, 'Well, he's not the best-looking fellow, but he's brave, and by God he's honest, and he's honorable, and he has courage—and I'm going to give him my business.'

"I don't care if it's a military action or if it's just life, you take a disadvantage, and you turn it into an advantage. That is what you do. Because you have to, goddammit."

He sat down, and for a minute, he was quiet. Then he said, "You know, that camera you have on that magnolia tree—that's a really good camera."

I patted him on the shoulder.

"You can be a troll if you want to, but that's not what you're intended to be. You're intended to be, from the moment you're born, a free-thinking son of a bitching fighting American. Someday you and me, we'll have lunch at the VFW, and I'll introduce you to the men there. We'll fix you up with a job or a business. You'll see."

And now, in spite of all that, I'm a crook, and I'm in cahoots with a republican. This is going to take some getting used to.

***

I've wondered why Franz Junior can't send a check in the mail like regular people do. It must be that he wanted to torture and humiliate his son, making him come in the darkness to the house mailbox as if he was a disgraceful monster. Then when young Patrick started hitting on him for money, maybe Patrick kept doing the same thing, as if he'd turned the tables on Franz.

But the weather turned into some nighttime rain storms, and when the first of the month came, I wondered if Patrick enjoyed coming to the mailboxes in the rain. It must have been worth it, though, when you think of how much every year Patrick was taking from Franz. I had no idea what kind of car he had or where his house was located. He wanted to keep all that to himself. I didn't press him on it.

For a couple of days after the first day of the new month, it was quiet. On that second evening, I fell asleep, dreaming I was aboard a freighter. Perhaps it was the *Cabrel*. It was sunny, with moderate swells, and I could sense the ship moving and hear her engines pounding. It was a pleasant dream, and I didn't like coming away from it, but I had to because I realized it was pounding on that front French door I was actually hearing.

It was the young couple who lived in their trailer pulled up next to Franz's house. They were knocking on that door frantically. The young woman's hair was a mess, and I got the impression she might have been ready for bed and had changed into jeans and a top hastily. She had frightened eyes but was in better shape than her young husband. His arms and legs were trembling. They had gotten used to the arguments, but tonight Franz and Madge got into a real physical fight. It sounded so bad the couple peered into windows, and then they entered the house. They found Franz had Madge down on the floor. He was punching and kicking her.

That unnerved them so much they fled in their car to come ask that 911 be called. I offered them the phone to make that call, but they wanted *me* to do the calling. Scared to death of their landlords.

I made the call. The wife kept saying loudly, so the dispatcher could hear, "She's probably dead by now!" I guess 911 got the message.

The couple didn't want to go back, but I insisted because when the police arrived, they needed to be there to talk to them. I went ahead of them in my Jeep, not the best transportation in bad weather.

They weren't going into the house. I was damp and unsure of myself, but I went in. The two combatants had stopped fighting. Now they were sitting far apart. Franz had some strange wrinkles and a few tears on his collared shirt, but otherwise he was fine. Madge, not so much so. But she was eager to talk.

Those two people from the trailer? She said they'd heard a TV show that was too loud. There'd been no fight. She had a wow of a black eye, and she had a story for that. Seems she was in the kitchen, and there was a cabinet door that was partly open, just at eye level. When she turned suddenly, the corner of that cabinet door had caught her eye in just the worst possible spot. That was her story, and when the police came, she stuck with that, telling it several times. She could walk, though she seemed to be in pain. No, she would not press charges. Nothing happened. No, she would not go to the hospital.

So Franz was safe. Nothing changed. Well, one thing did. The couple wanted me to stick around while they got ready to leave. They needed to disconnect their trailer from the house electricity, for one thing. Once they were ready, the young woman drove their car, and the fellow drove the trailer, and they escaped.

Franz watched everything from his doorway, his drink in hand. It seemed to me he had a sarcastic look on his face. I knew he was glad to see them go. I bet he had no idea what was going through my mind.

There are so many old mines out in the desert. Those deep holes are still uncovered, never closed, never visited by anyone unless you're some poor soul who blundered into one with your recreational vehicle. How easy it would be to drop Franz Junior into one of those old mines. Maybe beat the tar out of him first.

How sweet it would be if that drink he was first sipping and then swishing around as he smirked at me could turn out to be his last.

***

Carol has an old-fashioned glider on her patio, and she and I were sitting on that, swinging back and forth a little. She's mixed lemonade with sweetened iced tea, and although I think that's a sin, it is kind of tasty, so I'm enjoying it. She's shown me photos of her late husband. He had dark hair and dark brown eyes, and those eyes were twinkling with laughter. Carol said he always found something to laugh about.

"He was always into doing something or other, couldn't sit still. He'd get involved with projects for the neighbors if he ran out of fix-it things at home. I spent a lot of time missing him before I found ways of getting around that."

My appearance isn't similar to that good-natured man at all. I have bushy eyebrows, and I've been told I look a little forbidding. I think I'm the gentlest heart of all, but maybe not.

Maybe others see me as a cold, old bastard. If Carol has discovered some way of not missing somebody you loved, I'm for it.

"And what ways do you mean, getting around that?"

She thought for a minute. "Well, it's the first bird you hear twittering at dawn, for one thing."

"Okay, for me, that could be how Stinker wags his tail every morning."

"Or, it's reading a book in bed snug and warm in winter or in summer when there's a storm outside."

"For me, that could be sitting at the bar at the VFW."

"Or it could be getting a phone call from a friend."

"Having a friend give me a hug and kissing my ear."

That made her pause, and I could sense she was blushing a little. So I pushed my luck a little more.

"I like hugs, too. I'd like to give you a hug right now if that's all right."

Seems that it was. I hugged her, pulling her close to me as we sat there. I kissed her ear, her nose, and her lips.

"That's so you know you're a lovely woman with a ways still to go," I whispered.

My arms were around her. I felt her tremble when I said that.

Hot damn. I've still got it.

**

For a few days, it was peaceful. We got a lot of thunderstorms, and I did some thinking. Mostly, what I thought about was the me I used to be compared to the me that is today. I was late teens when I joined the service, and by my mid-twenties, I had convinced myself there were things that were worth any chances you had to take. Things like volunteering and not caring that much about myself. Like being dropped into the jungle with my translator and some other guy to meet a person who was eager to talk and then having to get out of there fast, depending on someone who was leading you out, who could have been turning us over to an enemy for all I knew. I was careless with my life, and I still have some nightmares about getting lost in dense jungle. What kind of life would that have been for Jenny? Would I have been more cautious if she had married me? I think about how her father doubted that military life would have been good for her. Maybe he really doubted if *I* would have been good for her.

It makes me angry; I'm so unwilling to take chances any more. Now I'm slow to make moves. I wish I could still be a troublemaker, but then I think, *hell, it's too much trouble to make trouble.*

***

It wasn't even dark yet.

There was an uneven hard knocking at the front of the house. Even as I approached that door, I could see it was Franz Junior standing there unsteadily. He was leaning against the doorway as much as he was standing in front of it. He must have started his drinking earlier than usual. He was vulnerable.

It would be so easy to kill him.

I opened the door.

"You almost got me carted off! Hadn't been for Madge standin' up for me, would've happened! You let those kids use your phone! Fine security you are! Puttin' the cops on me!" He rocked back on his heels, then straightened. "I'll get *him* carted off, tha's what! He's crazy, and he threatened me! Yes, that's true! I know people, and I'm calling them! On you, too. You're in on it. Both of you!"

He paused, breathing hard. A sly look came over his face, and he looked at me with eyes half closed.

"You know what he is, don't you?" He spoke that almost in a whisper.

"I know who he is," I replied. "I know how you treated him and Jenny. I know one other thing."

The tiger that had been growling in me stirred. I grasped him by his collar. I held him still as I put my face so close to his I could feel his breath as he tried to pull away. He must have known, then, a tiger had him. I had my mouth so close to his ear.

"I know the final thing. That thing you thought was finished and over with has come back on you and is going to eat you up alive."

Then I pushed him away from me, completely out the door. I shut it and locked it. He knocked a few more times. Then he staggered off to his car, I supposed, for I heard it when he drove off.

I had kept to that part of me that clings to reason and hope. The better part of me. I was to hear no more from him.

Young Pat was incredulous.

"Who doesn't have a cell phone these days? Why did that couple have to involve you?"

"Doesn't matter. I made the phone call for them. He's mad with me just because he wants to be. Let's hope he hasn't made any phone calls about you to anybody. Let's just hope. When he gets sober, maybe he'll forget all about that. I hope so."

I tried to put Franz out of my mind. He was off somewhere or in Delaware. He'd be back when he felt like it.

But then Madge called again. Oh, she was so alone. Please come because she was alone and she was scared that intruders would come when Franz wasn't there.

I didn't want to talk to her. She had a chance when the police were there to get away. But maybe she would know if he'd really made any phone calls. It would be a good thing to find out.

I had sense enough not to go alone. Ted wanted, all along, to see into that situation, and Terri and his daughter Misty shared his curiosity. The four of us went forth like crusaders. I was half afraid if I didn't go to her, Madge would show up at my door again as she had before.

***

Madge wasn't glad to see us. Maybe she wanted me to have come alone. She was at her stylish best, in spite of her one eye still looking sad.

"We two will check around outside," I told her, "and the girls here will keep you company while we do that."

"Yes, I'll be glad to help you," a young and attractive Misty said to her. Madge was surprised, and she visibly brightened.

"I'll help you get your things together so you can leave him," Misty continued. That must have startled Madge, for her false eyelashes fluttered till one of them fell forward over her bruised eye. Pitiful.

Terri told me later it was relentless. The conversation would be pleasant, and then it would get back to the same thing over and over as they peppered her with questions about her personal safety:

    Why didn't she press charges?

    Why didn't she leave him, at least for a while?

    Why wouldn't he marry her?

    How could she be sure he would provide for her in case something happened to him when he was off drinking so much?

    Did she have any kind of legal authority to make decisions for him if he got hurt?

    Oh, what a pity a nice respectable woman like her was being so ill-used by Franz.

    Madge made her position clear. She was never going to leave him. She'd have them know there was a will, and she was in it. Just her. Nobody else. Franz told her so. She was going to be well taken care of and then some.

    Terri said she told Madge, "Well, in that case, if it was a sure and certain thing, I would have my own personal finances; he'd better not beat up on me like he did on you. He'd be waking up with a new parting in his hair, put there by a frying pan, if he did that to me." But Terri didn't know how to approach the topic of phone calls, so she never got around to that. I learned nothing about any phone calls Franz might have made.

    As for Ted and me, patrolling around outside with our flashlights on, it was just a peaceful stroll. If you're looking for somebody, you don't let them know you're there, walking around with flashlights flip-flapping around. If Pat had been there, he was long gone when he saw us. It wasn't close to the first of a new month, anyway. Franz had been conditioned to always be handy when that date rolled around. And just prior to that was when Patrick came to call on them to make sure he got his money.

"Fat chance she's ever leaving him," Ted commented.

"No, none."

We assured Madge there was nobody around and that the cameras were recording our presence, front and back. And we left.

***

After that, when Madge found herself alone again, I guess she mulled things over.

When she couldn't find a will anywhere in the house, not in any file cabinets, or any closet or any trunk, or anywhere else, perhaps she called their local lawyer, if they had one, and then she must have called their local bank to see if there were any safety deposit boxes. When she got no results, finally, I'm guessing, she got around to calling the people she still knew from the glory days when she was somebody of importance in the corporate world of Delaware.

This is how I see what old Franz did. In my mind's eye, I see him preparing to go to Arizona. So he had a will prepared that left everything to Franz Junior. And, because his son was grown and newly-wed and was taking over, he had a second will prepared, one for his son, Franz Junior, to save him the trouble of doing it later. I'm thinking that happened, and that after Franz Junior signed papers, a corporate lawyer kept copies of those two wills. Anyway, Madge finally made contact with the right people. Yes, there was a will that left everything to Franz Junior. No, she wasn't in that will. There was a second will, though. That one was the will of Franz Junior, and she wasn't in that one, either.

But Jenny was.

***

I've heard some soldiers are forewarned about their coming deaths by a feeling it's just ahead. They know ahead of time they're going to die. I don't know if that's true or not. But remembering that made me think of Franz Junior. I wondered if he had any warning, any inkling at all, of what was waiting for him when he finally returned home. Did he imagine the sort of Fury that had been like an evil bread rising from its bowl, doubling and redoubling in size for the better part of a week? Speaking figuratively, Madge's fake eyelashes had been blown into the stratosphere when she learned she wasn't in any will.

However, she found one interesting thing in a bedroom closet. She found his Glock semi-automatic pistol and its ammo. What in the world a sissypants like Franz was doing with such a weapon is beyond me.

A determined future shooter, she got comfortable with it, the police later said, practicing her shooting in the desert at the rear of the house. How she was even able to pull the trigger is a mystery, for it takes some strength. I figure she would shoot with short bursts, then stop, and then do it over again. I don't know how she could be accurate with a Glock, either.

But maybe she worked on it with the persistence of a real western gunslinger, and when Franz entered his house, she tried to make his belly button a six-pointed star.

It must be admitted bullets were sprayed around and hit a lot of things besides Franz, but she managed to hit him with three of her shots. One was in his shoulder, at his back, as if he saw what was coming and tried to escape, and two were to his head, also from the rear, so he wasn't as fast as he needed to be.

One head shot wasn't so serious, but the other one put him down.

I give Madge credit for one thing; she did call 911 for him. But she didn't stick around. She, his pistol and its ammo, and God knows what else disappeared. The police were looking for her, of course, and eventually she would have to reappear, but for now, she was on the loose, which was worrisome since she liked to turn up at my place. And she wasn't happy with me. Like some soldier trembling in his boots, feeling he might be going to die, I had some bad feelings.

***

There wasn't much time to worry about Madge. Young Patrick must have been feeling lost and wondering how in the world he was going to get any money to live on when he heard about Franz being shot. Franz was alive but in intensive care in bad shape, and I guess Patrick decided to do something reckless and foolish. God bless him, he took a flight to Jacksonville, and then he rented a car and went to the beach. Then he sat there on that beach, and to quote him, he "went to work". And some troublesome work it was, born from a young brain that was crying out, I-don't-know-what's-going-to-happen-to-me. It brought me to my feet in dismay when I watched the evening news on TV and saw that a Russian sub was missing somewhere in the Atlantic. Only it wasn't really missing at all.

The Russians knew exactly where that sub was, and after the news broke, so did a lot of other people. The Russians knew every word that was going in and coming out of that sub, and so did others. The captain said nothing was working right, and they were lost, and his superiors kept saying no, you're not, here's your position, but the captain kept replying that couldn't be right, for they weren't anywhere near that position at all—and when he was told now you must go to the surface and run topside, the captain said that's what they had been doing for some time. Only they hadn't, you see, and weren't at all. And that's when I knew this was young Patrick's work. The sub finally surfaced in international waters far off New Jersey with a confused crew and a captain in trouble. They had been headed south. I amuse myself by thinking perhaps they were going to Jacksonville.

When he returned, and I saw him again, Patrick was delirious. "I thought I could do that, and I can! I did that! Hooray!" Well, hooray, hell. He'd forgotten the warnings I gave him earlier, and now it was time to remind him of what could happen.

"Listen to me, Patrick! If Franz did make some calls, and he could have, that's for sure, and then Franz got shot, and next comes this sub thing… it could mean trouble."

"Oh." Yeah, now he remembered.

"Like some federal agents come calling."

Now he was looking miserable.

"We have to keep quiet. Maybe he didn't call anybody. Maybe he got shot before he could. We have to hope. But don't do anything else, hear?"

He nodded, and I could tell he meant it.

"We just have to sit tight and be quiet. Maybe we'll be lucky. I think we'll be lucky. So don't worry. We're always lucky." Wrong.

***

I've always respected our federal agents, especially the FBI. I've never worked with any of them, but I've been told they're hard-working and well-trained. When they ask you a question, they probably already know the answer.

So when one of them appeared at my door just a few days after young Patrick returned, I felt as if my stomach dropped to my knees.

The FBI agent who came in and sat down was quietly friendly but serious. I figured he probably was right-handed – most people are – and under his left armpit, there might be a holster with a weapon in it. The casual way he sat with his suit jacket falling loose on the left meant he could reach a weapon easily. If he had one, that is.

He came at the reason for his being with me at once. The FBI had gotten some news from a couple of senators concerning the grandson of a prominent inventor. The father of that son expressed concern about the young man's sanity. He said his son was crazy, that he had threatened his father, had stolen some of his inventor grandfather's papers, and that he was a threat to the public's safety.

I had been mentioned, too. Since I was retired military, an officer once in security and intelligence, it was thought that a visit with me might save everybody time and effort. Maybe I could tell them a lot about this crazy grandson, crazy son. Maybe I could tell them where they could find that person, That crazy son and grandson, that is, if he was.

The business about stealing some pages of his grandfather's work was a new one to me, and I was conscious of pages young Pat had read to me lying on the table behind the sofa in a sloppy heap under an ashtray. I was suddenly glad I hadn't pressed Patrick about where his rented house was or where he kept his car—or, for that matter, what kind of car it was.

So what was one to say? Look in libraries? I was kind of stumped and didn't know exactly how to respond.

Stinker was lying sprawled in the seat of an upholstered wingback chair, and I was sorely disappointed in him. He hadn't sounded any alarm to let me know the FBI was arriving, and he had just lain there regarding the man from under his Scottie eyebrows. What the hell was wrong with my dog anyway?

But now, as I looked at him, he suddenly became interested in the French door nearest him, the one that served as my front door, where the agent had just entered a minute or so ago. Stinker stood up and stared. So somebody else was approaching.

Through the age-riddled curtain that hung at that door, I could see a figure coming up to it. It was Madge. Definitely Madge. I was suddenly thankful I always keep doors locked, that I'd locked that door right behind the agent after he entered.

Across her chest was a cross-over designer bag. Madge wouldn't be out in public unless she was in style. And in her right hand, raised and pressed against the door, I saw she had a gun.

"Gun," I said to the agent. And I suddenly remembered Madge's last name. It was Wilson. It's a good thing to remember the full name of somebody who's probably come looking to kill you.

"Excuse me?" said the agent.

"Gun," I said again, and I nodded toward the French door and rolled my eyes. I have since then realized it was brighter outside than it was in the room, so Madge couldn't really see in much at all, and that raggedy curtain was doing its job.

The agent looked at the figure pressed against the door, and I knew he could see there was a gun.

"Who's that?" he asked.

"I know you're in there!" Madge cried out. "Your car is in the carport! It's all your fault!"

"What's all your fault?"

"That's Madge! She's shot Franz, the father who complained—"

Stinker chose this moment to remember his guard duties. He began barking and growling with all the strength he had.

"So she thinks it's my fault she shot him. Well, that's how she sees things…"

I was beginning to warm up to the telling of all this. Madge was jiggling the handle of the French door. She could get in very easily at any door or window by using the butt of the gun to smash a pane or by shooting one out, but she didn't want to do that. She was a fussy one, like Franz, and wanted to keep things perfect, remember? So she wanted a door or window that wasn't locked. Something open.

"How's anything your fault?"

Now she was at the French doors on the other side of the fireplace. Those two doors never got opened or used. Lots of luck opening them.

"Well, there was this couple who were supposed to help keep those two calmed, but Madge and Franz got into a fight, see, and they had to call 911, and so she and Franz held that against me. Well… she's nuts, that's all."

Now she was at a window at the other side of the room. I'm air conditioned to the Arizona hilt, so that wasn't going to open, either. The FBI agent was turning his body, following her movement around the side of the house.

"You come out here! It's your fault! You and your cameras!"

"Cameras?"

Every time she shouted, Stinker let loose some more, and it was hard to talk over him.

"Well, yes, they wanted security, you see. They blame me for their trouble with the son."

"And what's the trouble with the son?"

The tone of the agent's voice was changing a little bit, and I wondered if he might not be re-thinking who was crazy and who wasn't.

"Nothing... he was born... well, looking different, and they hated him from that minute on—nothing wrong with him." Then I added a lie, an out-and-out lie. I don't know why. It just seemed to fit in. "He's... hiding from them. Yes, just hiding from them."

She was jiggling the handle of the back door. The agent stood up. He knew now there was a back door. He took out from under his left armpit a respectable weapon, something that got my attention.

"I moved to the wall and peered around it, because I could see Stinker standing on his chair cushion looking in the direction of the back of the house, and he had the strangest expression on his doggie face. He left his comfy chair and approached that thing he was seeing, walking gingerly.

I was still dribbling words as I looked.

"Hiding... from... them... yes."

Madge had discovered Stinker's pet door. What made her think this was a good idea is beyond me. She was lying prone on the cement walk that led to the back patio, and she had put her arm holding that gun into the room through the pet door.

Stinker must have thought it looked like a snake with a big snake head. What I saw, to my horror, was a Glock weapon, although it looked a little smaller than the others I had ever fired. I didn't know right then how she had been practicing with that weapon. I felt the hair on the back of my neck rise up. Police and military sometimes use a Glock. I know how fast that firepower is.

As I peered, I could see one eye of hers looking up at me.

"Ha! I see you!" she declared. And that is when she opened fire. Hell broke loose. Stinker retreated to a corner. She was blocking the only exit he had. The Glock bursts were tearing apart the very French door she had been so finicky about a little while ago. She also was spraying parts of the ceiling. I was at the farthest-off French doors, the ones you can't get to open unless you're pulling really hard, and believe me, I was, but they weren't budging. The only person who did something smart was the agent. He headed for the back door.

You run out of ammo pretty fast with a Glock, and now I could tell she was reloading. So that purse was – aha! – full of ammo magazines. I was peering around the wall again. She got reloaded and had her arm back in through the pet door again.

Stinker made a gutsy run for my side of the room just as the agent said to her, "Put the gun down! Don't make me shoot you!"

I will always remember what that silly woman said. Here you are, lying on the ground, and there's a man standing over you, and he has a gun, and he has the drop on you. I guess because she was ready to shoot again and had her arm already in the pet door, she figured she was in charge. Who knows?

"Now, who the hell are you?" That's what she said to him, and she opened fire again. The agent made good his threat. He shot her in her thigh and in her ass.

That's not a good place to shoot somebody, but he could have shot her somewhere else and killed her, you know. She screamed and dropped the gun inside the room, and I ran and moved it out of her reach. If she'd pulled her arm back out of the pet door still holding that gun, it might have been a tragic matter for her. I think she was lucky.

I stayed there outside for a while, watching as Madge got taken off to the hospital, the same place where her poor victim lay. "He shot me in my behind," she whimpered in a little girl voice.

***

Back where we began our conversation, I found the FBI agent. He was sitting primly, just as quietly as before. I guess he used the time he had there alone to take photos of those pages that were on the table under that ash tray. It made me a little angry.

"He's not crazy," I said, standing over the pages. "He's a person who's patriotic and just needs to be treated fairly. I don't know where his house is or where he keeps his car, or what kind of car it is. I haven't pressed him on that, because sometimes you take things slow when you're trying to build up the confidence of that person and get him to trust you after all the years of cruelty he's had. You didn't have time to photograph all the pages. That's because some of those pages have writing on both sides, and I wasn't out there that long. You heard those sliding glass doors that go to the patio squeak, so you just fixed the pile up and put the ash tray back. I can tell you're former military. When I put those pages on that table, they were all jumbled up because I was in a hurry to lie down there. You put them in a nice neat pile without thinking because you're always going to be military, no matter what, and you forgot they weren't neat before. So you're not perfect, Mister Agent."

His eyes told me he knew I was right. He sort of smiled.

"Those pages were important to young Pat. He told me what they said about what his grandfather thought modern warfare could become. He understands everything his grandfather did or thought about. He's that good. It's a moot thing about his 'stealing' any pages, though. He's the only heir, and his father died in the hospital last night. So I think those pages of his grandfather's belong to him. What do *you* think?"

Before he left, I handed him the Glock.

"I never saw anything like this before. It's smaller," I said.

He inspected it. "Oh, yeah, a 19. Shorter barrel, but 17 magazine can be used for it. She sure shot the hell out of this place." He laughed.

Half of the front of my house, and a demolished door. I wasn't laughing.

He turned the weapon over to the local law because it had been used in an attempt to kill me, and, of course, it turned out to have been used on Franz Junior.

We shook hands, and he left. I wish I could have read his written report.

I have to remember to fix those sliding glass doors out to the patio, so they don't make any noise.

Somebody is going to be reading the photo copies of those pages, and they're really going to want to see all the rest of what was written.

***

For about a week, I didn't hear a word from young Patrick. I had no way to get in touch with him. So I had to wait patiently. Finally, he showed up.

By then, I'd been wondering what made Madge explode, and I figured old Franz probably had a will. A sort of forlorn hope plan formed in my mind. I had a psychiatrist whose name I just pulled out of the yellow pages come from central Arizona to have a session or two with Pat, and I paid for her report that he was sane. I found out from one of the VFW fellows the name of a young lawyer, a fellow called Howard ("Howie") Lankford. Everybody said he was a smart young guy.

I met with him. I gave him my typed account of what happened to young Patrick, and his eyes widened as he read it, which I took as a good thing, for I think it meant he was interested. I'd been told he liked to chew gum when he sat thinking; he was doing that. The eyes showed interest again when I said Pat was the only heir if there was a will. I didn't know about Franz Junior, but I was pretty sure old Franz had left a will. But I couldn't be positive.

Young Howie leaned back in his chair and asked if there was some way this young Franz Patrick Gephardt the Third could prove he was who he said he was, and when I told him there was a birth certificate in Pat's possession, he smiled. He was chewing his gum happily.

Then, as he flipped through pages of what I'd typed, glancing and pausing here and there, he asked what the name of the bank was.

"Bank?"

"Yes, you know. The bank those checks were written on, the checks left in those mailboxes. I'll need that."

The problem, I told him, was that if the only will was that

of old Franz, when he left to live in Arizona, young Pat hadn't been born yet, so unless his will was written later on, Pat wouldn't even be mentioned in it. His smile didn't waver.

What was more, we would be dealing with a large corporation that always had taken good care of the grandfather and the son, and they probably wouldn't believe or even want to hear about the child abuse Pat suffered. I felt that should give Pat an edge in inheriting anything, but they probably wouldn't want to think so. I didn't want to involve Pat until there was a chance he could benefit. He'd had enough suffering.

So, was Howie interested? We'd go to Delaware, and we'd have to go see Mrs. Lightfoot and anybody else who could back up the abuse. I told him that.

And before he met him, he needed to know Pat was a most unattractive fellow, physically.

"Most of my clients are unattractive people, Mr. Monahan, in one way or another. That's why they need me. If it's all that bad, why are you interested in helping him?"

"He's really an intelligent, solid person." And then I added the truth, which I figured most people knew. "I loved his mother. That bastard Franz caused her suicide. I see Jenny in her son. What I like is that he always bounces back. He has courage."

For the first time, he really looked at me. He quit chewing his gum. Judging me, I guess.

"You interested or not." I needed an answer.

"Definitely. We're going to Wilmington. I hope we can stay at the Hotel DuPont. They've got some wonderful paintings there in their Brandywine Room. So my father told me."

"I have a feeling you're going to be expensive."

"Only when I win. And I will win."

***

Maybe that lawyer was certain about how things would go, but I wasn't, not so much. When I finally got to sit down and talk with young Pat, he looked worn out. I could tell he was uncertain about what the future held for him.

"I want you to move in with Stinker and me," I told him. "I've got that extra bedroom. I'll pay the penalty for breaking your rental lease. Furniture and stuff there isn't yours, right?"

He was surprised, "No, not mine."

"Good. There's plenty of room in the carport for your car, too. I'll pay a couple of months ahead because you're going to be using it to do a job search. Insurance paid up? No tickets?"

"No, no tickets. Everything's okay." I could almost feel the tension lifting off him.

"You're going to be just fine. Sooner or later, you'll find what suits you best. Meantime, pretty soon, go down to Mr. Rob's garage and have the car tended to. Get anything it needs done. I'll pay for that, too."

Tentatively, he smiled. Of course, because I was doing for him the things a parent would want to do. He never had that before.

But now I stretched it thin. "Listen, because this is important. The men at the VFW are supportive. They've been collecting possible job openings for you. So I'm asking for a favor. Terri and Carol got you some new clothes … they're on the bed in what's your room. So go shower and get dressed, and we'll go to the VFW."

Now he was distressed, frowning. But he went to shower anyway, much to my relief. And he came out wearing those new clothes. I was sure of the sizes, and the two women knew what was cool. He was frowning because he hated meeting people and dealing with the stares he got at his poor face.

"You look nice, so don't worry about it," I said. "If people stare, it's that goatee that's doing it. It isn't going anywhere. I'd shave that thing off pretty soon."

At the VFW, no staring happened. They shook his hand. They told him what they'd heard about jobs. Slips of paper, cards with phone numbers on them, smiles, and free beers, that's what he got.

Just before we left, one older veteran came close, touched his shoulder and said, "You must be Colonel Monahan's boy." That startled him, I could tell, but I think it pleased Pat.

When we got back to the house, he got some news he didn't like. The fact that a lawyer and I would be going to Delaware to see about any will that might benefit him, and he would not be going with us, made him angry.

"Well, why not me, too?" he demanded to know.

"If we aren't successful, I don't want you to see me sitting there crying. If the news is good, we'll call you before we leave to come back home. Carol's going to come cook for you and Stinker, and you two just keep the home place safe. A couple of days, time for Mr. Lawyer to "round up his horses", so to speak, and we'll go. It shouldn't take long. You have to back me up on this. I'm counting on you."

"Won't you even tell me who the lawyer is?"

"If he wins, I will." I tried to be funny.

***

A couple of days later, Carol drove me to the airport. Patrick saw me off with a smile. I like that about him, how he stands when the wind blows. And his goatee was gone. Howie, the lawyer, met me at the airport. He slept most of the way on the plane. So either he was not worth much, or he was pretty damn sure of himself. I noticed he chewed his gum furiously when he was looking over his paperwork.

Howie (that's what he said I should call him, possibly because I reminded him of his dad or his grandfather) had the address, and we went first to the estate of what had been home to old Franz and Mickey. There were new owners now, but he'd already been in touch with them, and they had some names and phone numbers of former staff. Howie got in touch with a former chef who helped us.

Then we went to Meta Lightfoot's home. She gave us an earful. A long list of awful things, not only for the little boy she remembered so well, but also for his mother.

And she gave us one other thing that made both of us grateful to her. When Franz Junior, at the end of one awful week of experimenting, dipped a towel in ice water and wrapped it around his little boy's head to relieve the boy's pain, the way that poor child looked made Meta so angry, she took a photograph of him. She still had that photo, and now she gave it to us. She found the boy suffering that morning, and it showed on his face. He looked like crap. There were dark circles under those haunted eyes, and the towel was all crooked around his head.

Oh, yes, that photo was to be a blessing.

Only one last day to organize, and then we strutted our stuff.

The corporation board of directors wasn't so impressed with us. Yes, as Howie had found, there were two wills. One had Franz Junior to inherit, and the other had Jenny, and since neither one of them mentioned Franz Patrick Gephardt the Third, what was the hubbub all about, anyway? Maybe he wasn't even really Franz Junior's son.

Howie swung into action. Oh, he was that son, indeed, and here was a birth certificate that said so, and since both the father and the mother were mentioned as heirs, the son of these two people, if he was ignored, brought consequences into the room. Sometimes, Howie said, things don't have to be written down in birth certificates to cause consequences. If there is no justice for an heir, no resolution, for example, consequences occur.

All the men around that table had been made aware of the abuses heaped on Franz Patrick Gephardt the Third from when he was just a little boy until he was in his teens. True, stressed Howie, the corporation didn't mean to cause cruelty, but it did happen. And now the corporation must protect itself from any consequences. Think now of all the companies that depended on this corporation for their financial security. And now Howie named some of those companies. Yes, one manufactured children's clothing, another produced baby foods, and another made diapers. Could this board of directors guess how many of those companies would bail out if they heard of a lawsuit against the corporation because of child abuse happening during some experiments authorized and condoned by the corporation? How many of those companies would go hook up with some other corporation?

One of the board members, a handsome man, said in a bored tone of voice, "You don't have any real proof of such abuse, now, do you?" It wasn't really a question. "We just have his word for it and yours."

Now Howie produced the written page from the former

chef, and he passed copies of that to each board member and told them the chef recalled humiliation and physical pain, and he could give other names that would vouch for the same thing.

Copies of Meta Lightfoot's typed account got passed out, too. Howie described how the experiments went on for a week at a time, month after month for years, and how it affected the child. He also mentioned that it was the Gephardt name that was at stake, for it was the cruel father who wanted that poor child dead or put away in some institution. So many of those profitable patents were linked with the name "Gephardt". What a shame to dishonor the name. It wasn't the abused boy who was insane, but instead, the insane one was the father.

He passed around to each of them copies of that photo. Those comfortable men were staring down at something that was most uncomfortable to see.

And then came Howie's sword thrust to the heart.

"But you gentlemen have been acknowledging Franz Patrick Gephardt the Third already, for years, as a matter of fact. One of your corporate lawyers" – and he named the man – "has been instructing your bank" – and he named the bank – "to be sure to honor the checks Franz Junior wrote each month because those monthly checks, written out to Franz Patrick Gephardt the Third, were for his *son*. Sometimes these were specified for living expenses, and sometimes they were specified for educational expenses. In any case, they were to be honored by your bank because those checks were for his *son*. And those payments went on for years. Now is the corporation proposing to deny the *son* after all those years of supporting him?"

Howie gave out the bank manager's statement that those checks were designated to be cashed by the *son*, and that *son* was Franz Patrick Gephardt the Third.

Finally, Howie turned to the man who looked like an ambassador. He knew his name. "Well, Mr. Reich, do you want to come to the dance with me, or shall we fight in court?" That was what he said.

There was some whispering, but all the talking was over, and they knew it.

"What do you want from us?" That was what was said.

I spoke up then. "Whatever the father was getting, the son gets. And that's for his lifetime. Also, the legal costs—that cost will be submitted to this board by Mr. Howard Lankford here. The son needs financial help right away. He has no other income."

"You'll give us all this you have here?"

I looked at Howie. He nodded.

"Fine. Once we see payments to young Patrick kicking in, and everything is on paper and certain." Just like that. It was as easy as saying Patty Cake, Patty Cake, Baker's Man.

When we left, I stopped at the door.

"You might want to listen to him, by the way. He's as brilliant as his grandfather but more sociable. And he's just as smart as his father but without the cruelty. He should be able to come into this board room. It was my father and his grandfather who started this corporation."

***

We were staying at the Hotel DuPont. We ate on the lowest level in the Brandywine Room. There were paintings everywhere, one in every booth and one immense painting over the fireplace. Young Howie impressed me. He didn't talk at all.

He just went around from booth to booth, sometimes sitting to look at a painting, sometimes just standing there, and ending up at the fireplace, admiring. Finally, he joined me where I was sitting in my booth with, overhead on the wall, a painting of a pirate hunkered down all alone on a beach.

He pointed at the painting. "Have you ever been marooned?" he asked.

"For years," I answered. "You did a good job," I added. "You bill the corporation, and then, after Patrick's had time to accumulate some money, he'll pay you again under the table. I would go to jail if necessary to do that double dipping because you just made good an awful thing."

Before we left the next morning, I called home. Carol answered. "Tell Pat he's going to like it," I told her.

Howie drove me home from the airport. I'd forgotten how the front of my place looked. He gave a skeptical look at the plywood covering where the French door used to be.

"What the hell happened to your house?" he asked, chewing away.

"Well, this woman wanted me, and when I wouldn't let her in, she became violent," I said. Nodding, I added, "That's true. True story." He was chewing his gum, sort of believing me. "But there was this FBI guy here, and he shot her in the ass."

Now he laughed. "Oh, yeah. You're so attractive to females, the FBI has to be called in. Women want you. They're after you." He laughed so hard I could see his chewing gum.

The memory of those eyes peering at me caught up with me. I was serious now when I said to him, "Howie, I just want somebody to explain to me how it is my ugly face can cause somebody to shoot at me through a dog door. How did the world get that crazy nuts? Am I really that awful?

"Well," I said, and I was sincere now as I spoke, "at least I remembered her name."

I left him not chewing his gum, eyes narrowed, looking at me thoughtfully.

For the next two days, I felt like a conquering king. Surely, this was the solution for everything. All would be peaceful and calm.

Wrong.

***

I don't like it when the military screws up, and they screwed up royally with what they did at my house. It was a military operation, even though that FBI fellow who had been here before was in on it. A tough-looking special ops sort was also part of it, and that says it all. Obviously, they were interested in what old Franz thought modern warfare could become, and they wanted to see all of it, all those pages that didn't get photographed.

I was thoughtless. I got involved with whether or not there was a will, and I forgot those few pages under the ashtray on that table.

They probably didn't know young Pat was living with me. His car wasn't in the carport because it was at the garage, and it wasn't ready for him to go get it yet. Only my car was there.

Stinker and young Pat were on the sofa; he was playing those war games on the TV. I was going to walk up to Carol's house, just a few houses away on the paved road, to have dinner with her. Since Pat was so involved with that game, I offered to bring some dinner back to him, and that was fine. So off I went.

They probably watched me walking away. The idea was they would enter, take the pages, and get out quickly. Nobody to stop them, and nobody hurt.

They didn't want to park out in front, so they went into the service road, turned around there and ended up on that road in the exact best spot for the camera on the tree to pick them up. It was daytime, so now there was no sudden telltale flash to give the camera away. The camera took two photographs of them, and their operation started turning into the Keystone Cops.

They got a surprise when they found young Pat there, and I could see there was a struggle. The sofa was pulled away at an odd angle, so he protested. Maybe that rattled them. Under that same table where those few pages were located was the medium-sized trunk that held all of old Franz's journals and notes. It was under my mother's table runner, and that sort of disguised it. But it was there, free for the taking, and one would think they would have seen it. They didn't.

Stinker bit somebody, for there was blood under his chin. I found him in the storage closet. He was barking, and that might have been when they said to themselves, well, what the heck, take this guy Patrick with us, too. He understands this stuff and can explain it. So kidnapping, in addition to stealing, right?

The camera took two more photographs of them as the military fellow pushed a frightened Patrick into their car. There were three of them, so Patrick didn't have much chance of getting away. The second photo taken then showed a heavy-set man falling down, so their getaway got slowed down. He had a handkerchief or something around his hand, so I'm guessing he's the one who got bitten.

I was standing outside at the back of Carol's place. I heard a dog barking, and it sounded like Stinker to me. So I went to the front of her house, and I saw their car as it left the service road. It came out onto the paved road and headed north.

I called Howie Lankford, and then I ran off those four photographs. Carol came to the house to be moral support, and I needed it because I was hopping mad. Here was a federal agent, a military man, and God knows what the falling-down guy was coming into my house, trespassing, stealing, and kidnapping. Not exactly the American way of doing things. It was one long, cigar-smoking night.

But by dawn's light, there was a plan. Howie contacted a senator his family knew, one who would be up for re-election in a year or so, and an appointment was made for me to go speak with him. I went armed with my photographs. That led to what I really wanted: a chance to talk with some Pentagon officials who'd been shown those photographs before they'd see me.

I was thinking of some publicity and a lawsuit.

Patrick must have been wondering again what was going to happen to him, for it was almost a month before I got results. Pat was probably being held at Quantico or someplace nearby. Howie was with me at the meeting, but these military men weren't going to be intimidated by him, a civilian lawyer, not by much, anyway. They weren't happy with how things went at my house, and those four photographs were embarrassing, especially when the FBI guy was wearing a red baseball cap.

"Oh," Carol said when she saw that. "He must have voted for Trump."

I wanted to speak to Patrick on the phone, and at first they said no, but I kept persisting about that, for I wanted to know he was all right, and finally, they let that happen.

While I was talking with young Pat, Howie gave each of those ten men a typed page that set out what I'd like to see happen. If I didn't have those photos, I wouldn't have been so bold. I had one other thing, though. I had all the rest of those journals and papers of old Franz. So, just let young Pat enlist in whatever branch of the service he thought would be best for him. There he could serve his country, explain all the experiments and written thoughts of his grandfather, and be safe himself. So much better than a lawsuit and embarrassing publicity, especially when you considered that smiling FBI man and his red cap.

Howie was quick to point out that when young Pat left the service or retired, all the things that were from old Franz would still belong to Pat and would leave with him.

I mean, no hard feelings. I made it clear I understood why they raided me. They wanted to protect their country, that's why.

One scowling medal-bedecked man broke into criticism loudly. "You think somebody like him can enlist? He's crazy, and he's a moron, and you can tell that just from looking at him!"

Howie was quick to produce the psychiatrist's statement to the contrary. He gave out copies of her statement about Pat's sanity.

"No, he's not," I said. "He's not crazy, and he's just the opposite of being a moron. He's a genius; that's what he really is. Bring in some of your own psychiatrists. Let them talk with him and then see what they think."

I couldn't say much more because I was suddenly so tired.

One of them had been looking at me intently. "I think I've heard of you. There was a Monahan who parachuted into the jungle in Vietnam, and he brought out three American captives. Was that you? It was, wasn't it?"

"That was a long time ago," I said. They got quiet and were looking at me funny.

They had it all wrong. To parachute into the jungle was insane. Binh and I only had to jump down two or three feet from the helicopter into the clearing below. Binh was a fine man, and I often wonder what happened to him after Saigon fell. But then he was my translator and my helper. The fellow from a remote village was waiting for us at the edge of the clearing.

Some think of this as heroic, but it turned out to be more of a swap-meet or some kind of bartering. There was lots of talking, especially from a woman named Chau. Binh said she was upset because a relative of hers in another village had her child killed by the North Vietnamese. That was because he was a child of the dust. That's what they called any child born of a Vietnamese woman and an American soldier father. Binh said those children were held in contempt and ended up in the dust of the city streets, so they called them the dust children. The woman, Chau, had such a child, and she had been dying his hair black so the little fellow would fit in. Binh said everyone in the village, just about, was related to everybody else, and when three Americans fell into their hands as captives, the village wanted to do some business about that.

Those three Americans, with their eyes big as saucers, fell into the hands of the villagers because when a rescue helicopter came to get the wounded and the survivors of an ambush, they were either too far out or too slow to make it to the rescue chopper. Instead, the villagers got them. So they were captives, but it wasn't the Cong that got them; it was the village.

The woman, Chau, made what she wanted clear to Binh, and he told it to me. The village would turn those men over if I would take her little son and promise I would get him into the United States. If I did promise, then her brother, the man who met us at the clearing, would lead all of us and the child to safety.

Of course, I promised.

"You can do this?" Binh asked.

"I dunno. I can try."

Chau gave her child something to drink that must have had something in it to make him sleepy. She whispered in his ear, and then we set off with him strapped to my back. He slept most of the way. It was one miserable trip, but maybe the child's being there kept the brother from selling us out, turning us over to the enemy, no matter what his sister wanted. I've thought about that.

We had one of the best command officers I ever knew, a man we called "Weasel", and I have no idea why he was called that. He was an unconventional man. He let me stay off base with the boy till a fake marriage certificate winged its way to me from, of all places, Puerto Rico. That gave me as the father and a Puerto Rican woman as the mother. It stated she went to Vietnam before the war, and she died there.

He gave me the paperwork that allowed me to take my "son" with me back to the states on board a military transport. Just about everything, every single thing that officer ever did, was the stuff courts-martial are made of.

An orphanage in Pennsylvania took in the little boy.

***

I didn't see any progress being made with these men. I found myself saying to them, "You think of me as being some kind of hero? The real heroes were there, but I wasn't one of them."

I figured we were about to be ushered out the door anyway.

"You want to know real heroes? How's about the woman who whispered to her little kid, 'Remember me, I am Pearl of the Palace, your mother,' when she might never see him again? And those children living in the streets, insulted every day? How's about those three captives who didn't understand a word of what was going on around them? Or Bihn, who never, never let me down, not once? Or Weasel, who saved my sorry ass more than once and is the reason I'm still alive?"

I stood up and gathered the photos together.

"And Jenny, who had a child who looked so awful people said he was crazy or a moron without ever even knowing him... she was a hero, too, for she loved him, and she saw how smart and devoted he really was. He had nobody... *nobody*... except her, and then she died.

"You want to know what I really was? Who I was? I was figuring I was already dead. Took any risk. Didn't matter. I just gave up and decided I'd gamble with life every chance I got. That's a hero?

"Come on, Howie, we might as well leave. They're tired of us. They're not going to listen."

Outside, Howie murmured sarcastically, "Well, that was nice."

The thing I remember most about that little boy is that he never cried.

***

It was after dark, late, when we got back from Washington. Howie didn't have much to say to me on the plane or in the car.

I regretted my little speech. It hadn't helped anything.

The French door had been repaired before I left, and now, even in the dark, I could see Carol must have had somebody stain or paint that new door so it matched the other one. And that old rusted-out mailbox that was on the side of the French door was gone.

Well, good, then.

When I let myself in, I noticed the old no-good curtains that once hung over those two sets of French doors were gone, and now there were some new, more substantial curtains. Looked like linen or something like that.

Nice.

I headed to the patio, more from habit than anything else, but I realized as soon as I stepped out that it was late, and I was just too tired to sit out there alone with that crazy rosebush. I backed off and went back into the kitchen. That was when I noticed the sliding glass doors weren't making that dumb noise any more.

What the hell?

There was a surprise in the bedroom. Carol was sleeping in my bed. She was "looking after things" here, but I didn't know she was sleeping in my bed. Also in the bed, sleeping on top of the covers, were Fatty Pants and Stinker. They were sleeping with her. Stinker knows damn good and well he's not supposed to do that.

Madge and those damn home wreckers had made my dog lose his senses.

I retreated to the living room, turned on one light, and lit up a cigar. She looked so little and feminine, curled up like that with her dark head on the pillow.

Get thee behind me, Satan.

So tomorrow would be another day, and I expected Howie would call me. I hoped so, anyway, for there was something I wanted young Patrick to do.

I became aware Carol was standing at the bedroom door. She was wearing shorty pee-jays, and she was not looking like a kid any more... but she did look sleepy, and maybe a little out of sorts.

"I thought I smelled your smoke," she said. "Have you been back long? Why didn't you just come to bed?"

"Ah... I didn't want to wake you up."

"Don't be silly. The dogs and I will feel much safer when you're in bed with us." She turned and went back into the bedroom.

I have never before slept in a bed with Carol, though I have imagined doing that. Here was a romantic invitation, if there ever was one. She and *the Dogs* would feel safer if I came to bed. "Safer" is not what I want a woman to feel when I come on to her and get in bed with her. And dogs don't need to be anywhere near. I'm a tall person, and so I had to sleep in a diagonal position so I could get in without making everybody move about.

Her hair smelled good.

One of those dogs snores.

In the morning, she asked how the trip to Washington turned out. Not so good, I admitted. With my coffee came word she had taken that old mailbox down herself. She also had stained the French door herself. And although she had bought those curtains from a store, she had hemmed them, so they were just the right length. *And* she had fixed that noisy sliding glass door. How did she do that? With a bar of soap. Evidently, if you can find where the noise spot is and if you rub soap on that place, it fixes it.

So I'm feeling inadequate in every way this morning. One good thing: if anybody ever asks me if I've slept with Carol, I can say yes.

I could have gone into the other bedroom, for I do have two, and young Patrick wasn't here. But that would have hurt her feelings. That sounds idiotic even to me.

***

Around noon, Howie called. He was still miffed a little. "Nobody knew who those people were you were taking off about. A woman named 'Pearl of the Palace'? Where was all that coming from? That was scary—"

"It would take a whole lot more than that to scare those men—"

"Not them. Me. Patrick called me early this morning."

"Yes, I wanted him to. I figured he would give you the phone number for himself, so you can reach him. Did he do that?"

"Yes, he did, and what is this you want me to do now, make you his legal guardian? Are you interested in some of the money he's going to be getting?"

"No, no, something else. More important."

"Well, he's telling me, legal guardian and legal heir."

"Just the first part."

"Why, then?"

"So I can take legal action that would involve him. Like suing the federal government for negligence. Under the Federal Tort Claims Act, I can do that."

There was a pause. "You're a civilian. Do you know how

many hoops I would have to jump through—"

"It would be for me. I'm retired military. It was so easy to get at him here at my house. It could have been who knows? Russians, Isis, China, North Korea, who knows? If those photographs get out, why, me and my place, we could get hit again. But if Patrick was allowed to enlist, then Pat and all his grandfather's stuff, trunkful and all, would be held in government care and on government property. And he could be very helpful for national defense. More than they can guess."

"Listen to me, now. I know how you love the military, how you admire our government, our FBI, all that. Can you guess how many evil people there are in our government, even in our military and, yes, even in our FBI? Making a request of them is one thing, even making a complaint, but putting the screws to them is different. Not smart."

"What's wanted is such a small thing to them. Of no risk, but it has possible rewards. They'll cave. I could see how those four photographs affected them. Threaten the lawsuit and get in position to do it for real. Then threaten to release the photographs. And then suggest the solution – let Pat enlist, and tell them why, and – hey, make him a low-ranking officer. I'm counting on it. What I expect is they'll send a military lawyer to talk or at least talk on the phone. And then maybe that person will do the convincing. Better than trying to talk to ten of them. Let their lawyer do the talking. I expect that lawyer will get back to you. You lawyers like to talk to one another."

Another pause. "So you want two things: first, legal guardian, and then action against the government for negligence under the Federal Tort Claims Act. You're going to owe me a lot of money; you know that? I'm liable to end up with the crap being beaten out of me by some goons."

"I'm the only stob sticking up out of the water with a storm nearby, and somebody has to tie up his little boat on me because I'm all there is. Howie, have you ever played poker?"

"I'm no risk taker."

"Somebody told me you were a good lawyer. Shame it's not true, then."

"Very funny."

—and we hung up.

Maybe that red cap the FBI guy's wearing will do the trick.

***

There wasn't anything happening for days. Then, that old phone in the front of the house rang, and it wasn't what I had hoped, but it was good news just the same.

The corporation was going to start putting money into an account for Pat. Did he want the same bank as the previous checks were written on, or some different bank?

Same. Did I want to be designated as the person who would settle things if something happened to Franz Patrick Gephardt the Third, resulting in his death? No, have to be discussed later on about that.

About then, I heard some brief barking from the two dogs out on the patio and some kind of noise from the kitchen where Carol was. But there was more from the phone.

They'd been notified by Howie I'm the legal guardian. Did I want a separate account for me? No. Oh, and yes, the board of directors would like Pat to come attend some future meeting so they could get to know him. Yes, on that – and he would be in touch.

I hustled to the rear of the house. The two dogs weren't

barking now. They were stiff-legged, growling at a pyracantha bush that was growing at the back wall, hanging over it. And a groggy Carol, shaking her head, was picking herself off the floor where she'd fallen. She'd looked out the kitchen window and seen a small rattlesnake crawling into that bush. It was probably trying to get away from the dogs.

She's a woman who can handle anything. But not, evidently, snakes. Carol passed out, and when she fell, she hit her noggin on the floor so hard that already there was a sizable lump forming on her forehead. Looked painful, even from a distance.

The dogs had the good sense to stay well away from that bush. But was the snake still there or not? If it wasn't, then where was it?

A few houses away from hers, Carol knew a family that could help. The man would catch snakes, and then he would turn them free rather than kill them. When Carol called, he wasn't home, but his wife came.

She arrived with a long hooked pole and a lidded box. The dogs weren't so sure she was doing the right thing, poking that bush with her pole. I was close to sharing their opinion, but no snake came out, and she said it probably went over the wall.

She spotted that crack in the wall, the one I had been meaning to repair. Now it was even bigger, and I hadn't been paying any attention to it.

"It probably got in through there," she said. She peered over the wall. "Oh, there it is! It's going back into the arroyo."

What? Snakes lived there? "When Jim catches one, he lets it go back into its arroyo, the nearest one."

"No putting the snake into that box and letting it loose out in the desert?"

"No. They den up, but in the spring, they come out and move around. You just have to be careful of them."

That was when the phone rang again, and I left the kitchen and headed for the front of the house in case this was the phone call I wanted. I was still grappling with the news that snakes had been my neighbors all winter. Just one or two, I wondered, or many.

It was Howie. Yes, young Patrick was enlisting. The very next day, as a matter of fact. He'd chosen the Air Force. Howie had airplane tickets, and the military wanted me to bring the trunk with all old Franz's stuff in it.

"What made them change their minds?" I asked.

"You were right; they folded. Maybe they thought you could actually win a lawsuit. I don't know. I'll pick you up early."

"Just hang on a minute," I told him. Back in the kitchen, Carol was starting to look like a unicorn. Travel with her was out.

"Sorry. We've had a snake here, and Carol fell down. She's got a mean-looking bump on her head. I can't leave tomorrow. That snake could come back... I'm told he lives next door. So I'm going to be here, and she and I will fill that crack where he got in with cement."

So it was agreed that Howie would take the trunk, and he would see Pat, and I wouldn't get to, but I would write a note to give to him. It would have to do. There was that news from the corporation, too.

Well, well, well, then!

We stuck rags in that crack for the time being, and I went to the hardware store to get cement to use for the crack. Carol had the radio playing while we were sticking rags in there, and every now and then, I couldn't help it; I broke away and did my smarty pants dance—because what it meant was that both the young man and the trunk would be on government property, on a post, safer than here and doing good things for their country. It was satisfying.

I put some cold compresses on that forehead knot. It must have helped.

That night, Carol and I were behind a closed bedroom door, and the two dogs had to sleep someplace else.

***

Next morning, we worked together to fill in the crack with cement, and it was as if we knew things had changed. We sort of had an agreement now, to look after one another. No need to talk about it.

I made a resolution to read up on rattlesnakes.

Howie took some photographs of young Patrick a few weeks later, and he looked nice in his uniform. He had his military-looking sunglasses up on his crew-cut head. No goatee, no sideburns. What I saw was a man happy with the work he would be doing. He looked like a fellow who had something to contribute.

I had a chance to talk to him on the phone about a week after he enlisted, and I told him about the corporation board meeting that he was invited to attend, whenever he could arrange it. I gave him one piece of advice: walk in that board room as if you own the place. Because, in a way, you do.

***

I heard from Pat again, months after that, in an unusual way. It must have been around midnight. A phone rang, and it was one of those phones on Dad's work table, over against the wall. Those phones are on a different line altogether, and haven't been used in a long time, so it startled me and spooked me a little. It was as if Dad's ghost was calling. I struggled awake and answered it, sitting at Dad's work spot.

It was Pat. "Dad! I'm aboard the *Cabrel*! I'm taking care of her! I want you to know I'm aboard her! I had that board meeting! I'm writing you a letter about it! It's all good news!" Then he was talking indistinctly, maybe to the captain, for I heard his voice tell someone, "Let her talk to him!"

"Somebody wants to say Hello," he announced. There came blast after blast from the *Cabrel*. Carol sat up, awakened, wide-eyed. We talked some more, and then he told me he wanted to come home sometime soon when he had leave.

He'd been in Japan. "I have a lot to tell you!" he rejoiced.

Sometimes the heart does its own dance, even if you're sitting still, as I was. There were some more toots from the freighter even as we hung up.

"What's going on?" Carol asked.

"I've been adopted," I said. "This place is home, and he called me Dad."

"See?" I said after I got back in bed. "Isn't sleeping with me fun?"

But even after she slept, I was awake for a while, listening to the heart doing its own smarty thing.

***

After reading the letter about his first trip to GEPA

Corporation's spacious board meeting room, I'm guessing from its contents the members of the board had their curiosity about his unusual appearance satisfied. He wrote that he went to them wearing his uniform, not trying to look like anything other than himself. That is to say, he entered the room with confidence, and a little conceit, knowing he was prepared to tell them some things they needed to know.

Because he had been so ill-treated in his young life, he could never carry off arrogance. With Pat, I knew that would be impossible. For all of his life, arrogance wouldn't be his companion. Pride, maybe so. I couldn't imagine his being overbearing.

He came with a folder. He'd done his research. He knew all about problem number one – about freighters – before he talked to them. That was because he'd already talked to those who worked on board the freighters and the freighters' captains. The corporation had gotten rid of three freighters already. They were wondering how to get rid of the rest. What Pat knew was that scrap metal meant a lot of money, but keeping freighters in service was the better choice.

Pat addressed the problem. He told them it would be relatively easy to make their remaining freighters profitable again. I'm guessing he had their attention right away. All of a sudden, his unhandsome face wasn't important. What he had to say was.

There were now super-sized cargo ships taking over all the nautical shipping business. When those bad boys loaded on their freight, it came in containers that looked like railroad cars, and they stacked them below decks four stories deep. Of course, almost immediately, the smaller freighters lost all the large ports around the Pacific. Financially, this was a serious blow. It led to the loss of a whole fleet of smaller, older freighters. And GEPA wasn't the only corporation losing.

Now, they must concentrate on the hundreds of islands lying in all parts of the Pacific. Not for taking the island products out into the world, for those products were few – there was cocoa, palm oil, coconut oil, even some gold and copper – but there was so little of that, it wouldn't be profitable.

No, instead, Pat told them, they must concentrate on taking foodstuffs and supplies *into* the islands. There was an untapped market waiting for them there. Pat was convinced from what he'd found out just from contacting a few of those islands that there was a need for goods coming *in*. Some islands didn't have mooring berths or wharves of any kind, but even at those smaller islands, ships smaller than the huge freighters could come in alongside and offload goods.

Once the exact goods needed were identified and onloaded in Alaska, a freighter could trade with islands as it traveled to Australia, and there it would unload and onload even more foods and supplies. Then the freighter would head out to the far-flung islands, each time out making a profit.

Pat wanted to take one freighter on a trial run, from Alaska out to Australia, and then to the eastern Pacific, to prove such a venture could be profitable. He had a good idea, after talking with island authorities and officials, what sort of foods and supplies would be needed. He asked the board to let him take a freighter on a trial run.

He reminded them it wasn't unprofitable to get rid of a freighter, but it was eventually a loss. Trying to make the freighters they had left worthwhile was worth the gamble financially.

And here was one other thing: tourists. Traveling onboard a

freighter was becoming the new thing among tourists. Yes, the super cargo ships could take on passengers, too, but those people would be surrounded by cargo pretty much. Those giant ships were designed around cargo, period. That wasn't true on the older GEPA corporation freighters. Those passengers had cushier quarters, top deck and nowhere near cargo storage. He'd already been in touch with some tourist agencies and had been told passengers would certainly be interested.

There was interest, yes, there was. The directors said they would discuss it and let him know.

And this was when they ran into logical Pat.

Well, that was fine, but they only had a limited time to hem and haw around. The freighters were already losing them money, and if they didn't act in a timely way, that would get worse. There were a few things that had to be done before the weather got bad in the Pacific, and he wanted good weather for the trial run or trial runs, if there was to be more than one.

For one thing, some areas were getting picky about what kind of fuel a freighter was using. So extra fuel tanks had to be installed, and, along with that, the mechanisms needed to enable a freighter to switch from one fuel tank to a different type of fuel in a different fuel tank. They would have to be able to do that before they entered any area that was making fuel demands. That would take time and be expensive. It would have to be done immediately for his plan to work.

And there was one other thing. They needed to add stabilizers. On board a freighter, you feel every strong wave (and maybe even less strong waves, too).

If you added stabilizers, tourists would be much more comfortable, and it would be a good thing, too, if the passenger quarters were spruced up a bit. You know, a little paint.

Whatever was going to be done should be done before the weather turned against freighters. So they didn't have much time to make decisions.

And it was nice of them to invite him. He'd enjoyed it. He hoped they would decide to take action.

A little social conversation, and then goodbye. Out the door, leaving the folder and its contents behind.

Within a week, they contacted him. The work got done.

Whatever leave time he had, he was working on solving the freighter problems and making improvements. It was on that trial run he contacted me as they neared home port, realizing it was profitable.

He didn't get to see us much then, but I knew he was doing what he knew had to be done during whatever leave time he had. Once in a while, there's a person born who's like that.

He had us in his heart, those people waiting here, where he felt it was "home". He'd get back.

***

I have mixed feelings about "home" and where that is because, for some, more than one place is home. Today, Carol has gone to her place to take care of things there. I'm not sure what or why. I realize that place is home to her. That's where she lived for a long time with her husband, and it's where he died. It's not a place where I would want to live.

At some point, I'll certainly ask her to come live *here* and call *this* place home. It's home to Pat, and it's where my parents lived for such a long time. I'm not crazy about snakes in the arroyo or that brash rosebush out back, but it's still home, and I want her here. Not me there. Could be trouble ahead on that.

I was thinking about that as I stretched out on that beat-up, ever-so-comfortable sofa, my favorite resting spot. And, of course, I fell asleep there.

And then came that dream.

I'm skeptical about significant dreams. Or, at least, I was.

I was in a strangely beautiful world where the colors were brighter and better than here in this world. There were others with me, but I wasn't even looking at them. We were all sitting in a field on soft grasses. I've never had a dream before where I could smell sweet grasses, but that was the case this time. I could also sense clear water running nearby, and reeds and tall grasses growing alongside it.

Then, the terrain became rolling, and I was on a trail, once again with others. I saw Jenny ahead of me on that trail. She was standing still and looking up at me.

The sparkling eyes were the same, and that warm smile was familiar and sweet. Maybe the dead aren't supposed to talk to us. Maybe they can't, or it takes a super effort to do it. I knew what she was saying to me, nonetheless, even though it was a message without words.

She was telling me it was all right, that this was a place where there was no giving or getting into marriage, that it was all right for me to be happy, and she was saying thank you, thank you, and I have always loved you, Patrick Monahan.

I woke up abruptly.

All the rest of the day, that dream stuck with me. It wouldn't let me go. I was lost in Jenny's smile, wanting more of it.

Finally, after an evening beer or two, I came away from it. I'd seen where Jenny is now, the place she calls home.

***

It's hard to believe over a year has gone by. Pat came home on leave a couple of times. The last time, he made an interesting proposal. Come to Alaska, he said. The *Cabrel* would be coming back to her home port to stay a while. Weather was worsening, and this would be a good time to inspect the ship, make repairs, and give the old girl a rest. He wanted to introduce us to the captain and the people in the corporate Alaskan office.

"It'll be good," he said, "for you to be here when she comes in, to be where it all began. I'll be aboard her."

I don't remember a thing about Dutch Harbor, but if these people are supportive of the freighter and of Pat, I'll be glad to meet them.

It was a long trip, but Carol and I were on the wharf as the freighter approached, and the ship gave a blast to say she was glad to come into port. Even at a distance, I saw Pat waving. He was standing at a railing just below the bridge.

A young and attractive woman approached him. She was leading a group of tourists who were getting ready to debark. They had their luggage and belongings with them. I had the feeling she must have been hired to make the voyagers' trip pleasant, and perhaps she would even take them on some island tours. Probably she wouldn't be traveling shipboard again till this freighter, or another one was ready to head out. Now she gave Pat a hug. He grinned.

I remembered that a hug could sometimes start things, nice things.

Pat was looking casual, not in uniform, and very relaxed. I hope that meant the *Cabrel* had proved she could still be profitable.

Carol and I were covered up a little because it was windy and getting chilly on the wharf.

"I remember one time you said you hoped Pat could just be a regular, normal citizen," I reminded her. "It looks as if you were right."

Months earlier, she'd been compliant. She'd agreed to live at my place. That pleased me so much. Now it wasn't Liam and Mary's house. It was becoming Carol and Pat's house. Good decision on her part, I felt.

"Oh, I'm always right," she said teasingly. "Have I ever been wrong?"

"Maybe not so wrong, but I liked the old curtains in the front room. They let in so much light. Now those heavier curtains make the room darker."

All the tourists were coming away from the freighter, chatting with one another. They looked young.

Carol was smiling. "Oh, Pat," she said, "sometimes other women and I would walk our dogs just at dusk when it was beginning to get dark. You weren't aware of us outside. You would come into the front room, turn on lights, and there you would be with your cigar, standing there in your underwear."

It got worse.

"We enjoyed the show, for you were pretty sexy. One time, you turned and went to get a beer, we figured, or something like that, and we could see you had a hole in your drawers."

I was stunned.

"So, when I could see you were going to be my guy, I didn't want those other women enjoying the view, watching you standing there scratching yourself."

A plan started up in my brain – something about a rubber

snake under the sheets on her side of the bed.

"And when was this, when you decided I was going to be your guy?" I managed to say.

"Oh, when I realized I could never live anywhere without you… that I didn't want to, anyway, live anywhere away from you."

The snake plan disappeared.

***

What a lovely place it was where Pat took us to eat. There was a cozy fireplace, and some of the people who worked on the water were there. The good-looking girl who'd hugged Pat came in. I learned her name is Anna. She joined us. We had the best-tasting chowder, and she made a foursome, so we played cards. It was a good memory.

My dad once asked old Franz where he got all those ideas he developed. Franz said many of those ideas came to him as inspirations, as if they were sent from some other place. Maybe Patrick came like that, sent from somewhere else.

All I know is that once there was a little boy who was in a desperate situation. Now, that boy is a grown man who's living a good – a very good – life. And that is something I'm going to like getting used to.

The End